For J...
in fond memory of
distant days together.

A CHILD LEFT BEHIND

by
Phil Hutcheon

PRAISE FROM READERS' FAVORITE

"*A Child Left Behind* is an absolutely brilliant look at the life experiences of multiple different people and how even the tiniest thread can connect a patchwork of people into a common cause, . . . offering some of the most authentic dialogue I've read in a long, long time, as well as developing characters that we either would choose to ignore in real life or, at best, feel ambivalent toward. Instead we are forced to get to know them . . . through a character-driven story with an ambiguous final scene. And guess what? I loved it."

—Jamie Michele, ★★★★★

"The characters are as diverse as their memorable personalities. The author has . . . relayed a relevant and realistic tale of the many social and political issues surrounding people from diverse cultural backgrounds. The vicious circle of the poverty trap, the healthcare system, drug use, and violent crime, as well as their treatment at the hands of authorities, are just some of the subjects tackled. I loved the romantic relationship between Alicia and Eduardo and how it developed. The dialogue is very comical at times but there are also some very heartbreaking and brutal scenes. The story really places you in the shoes of someone who is struggling to find their own American dream in a hostile and very often unfair society."

—Lesley Jones, ★★★★★

"Any author prepared to tell his story from so many differing perspectives is an author of courage in my book.... Especially important was the veteran's reaction to returning to 'normal' society after a tour of Afghanistan with the Army Rangers. His no-nonsense approach to life was refreshing and yet he was still able to convey great empathy for other veterans who had struggled with their reintegration. This book . . . raises some excellent questions about who we are, what's important in life, and how to treat others. I enjoyed this read and just wish it had been double its size."

—Grant Leishman, ★★★★

"I found *A Child Left Behind* by Phil Hutcheon a complete page-turner. I'd been intrigued by the copious warnings at the beginning of the book that the content may offend sensitive readers. Was this book an honest look at the problems faced by many in modern society? Yes, it was and that was so refreshing. No, it's not politically correct but it's so candid it was a joy to read. . . .The characters leap off the page, the story kept me turning the pages, and I read the book in one sitting. . . . I loved the diversity of the people. I would love for this to be prescribed reading in schools – there are questions at the back for teachers to use in the classroom. I wish all literature was as open and honest as this book."

— Lucinda E Clarke, ★★★★★

Drawing on inspiration from Faulkner, *A Child Left Behind* by Phil Hutcheon is an irreverent narrative of five college students from varying backgrounds, mostly minority, that are following their dreams. Along with the students, the novel follows the lives of a few more diverse characters, creating an unputdownable novel. . . . Although each character is written in the first-person narrative, Hutcheon masterfully creates individual personalities, each with their own vernacular and background, most of whom I instantly fell in love with and admired. I came away from the story feeling inspired and oddly hopeful for our nation's future. Never before have I read a book with a first-person narrative in which the author has so excellently developed his story and characters. . . . This book should be a must-read for anyone on the fence concerning their country's issues and how they, as individuals, relate to the solutions. Challenging socially correct thinking, this novel may have the effect of altering one's political perspective."

—Ashley Elmore, ★★★★★

PRAISE FOR THE AUTHOR'S PREVIOUS NOVELS

WHERE TRIPLES GO TO DIE

". . . takes the reader on an emotional ride of a lifetime.... I couldn't put it down."

—Romuald Dzemo, *Readers' Favorite,* ★★★★★

". . . masterfully intertwines the lives of two men from different racial and socioeconomic backgrounds who are in different phases of life but are connected through their love of baseball."

—Christi Lyle-Rasheed, *Manhattan Book Review,* ★★★★★

". . . the nebbishy but subversively funny Wade makes an endearing ringmaster for this rollicking collegiate circus. An entertaining picaresque that mixes higher education and sports in hilariously inappropriate ways."

—*Kirkus Reviews*

"If you have any interest in fiction that is funny, topical, and insightful about college sports, gender, race, class, and academic issues, *Where Triples Go to Die* is a terrific book that fits the bill."

—Matt Wetstein, President, Cabrillo College

"A deftly written and inherently compelling novel by an author with a genuine flair for crafting memorably irreverent characters embedded in a narrative driven story of humor and pathos from first page to last, *Where Triples Go to Die* will linger in the mind and memory of the reader long after the book itself has been finished and set back upon the shelf. Unreservedly recommended for community library Contemporary Fiction collections . . . ."

—*Midwest Book Review*

DESPERATION PASSES

"Original, deftly crafted, and a truly memorable read from beginning to end, *Desperation Passes* is very highly recommended reading and establishes author Phil Hutcheon as an impressively talented novelist who will keep his thoroughly entertained readers looking eagerly toward his next book."

—*Midwest Book Review*

"You don't have to love football to get swept up in *Desperation Passes*. You probably don't even have to like football, because you'll quickly come to care deeply about Allenby and Wade, find yourself charmed by their clever repartee, and cheering them both on to come out on top."

—Molly Culbertson, *Manhattan Book Review*, ★★★★★

NOBODY ROOTS FOR GOLIATH

"Chronicling the battle against a host of life obstacles from bad grammar, drugs, and crime to paralysis-inducing political correctness, fickle lovers, and domestic violence, *Nobody Roots for Goliath* is a serious-minded, absorbing novel that reads like a true story because it draws so heavily upon harsh reality. Highly recommended."

—*Midwest Book Review*

"Phil Hutcheon has invented a new genre, a hilarious mix of sports, sex, and snarky dialog that just might entice a lost generation to put down their iPhones and Xboxes long enough to finish a book, with pleasure!"

—Diane Oren, Past President,
Academic Senate, Delta College

See more reviews of each novel at amazon.com/author/philhutcheon.

A CHILD LEFT BEHIND

by
Phil Hutcheon

MUDVILLE NINE BOOKS

an imprint of Tokay Press

Stockton, California

ISBN 978-0-9908466-1-1

I dedicate this book to the memory of Charles Otto Hansen, by his own proud account a "real dirt farmer," who fed the world; who loved the mountains and the ocean, animals of every kind (well, except perhaps coyotes), and his siblings' children as if we were his own; and who, in spite of unspeakable personal adversity, modeled without fail for those of us lucky enough to love him the irreplaceable virtues of hard work, integrity, common sense, compassion, and humor.

AND

To my students, who humble, educate, and inspire me every day with their efforts to pursue their dreams, often with few, if any, of the advantages that I have enjoyed in pursuing mine.

PART I: THE ABANDONMENT

"Life, misfortunes, isolation, abandonment, poverty, are battlefields that have their heroes—obscure heroes, sometimes greater than the illustrious ones."

—Victor Hugo, *Les Misérables,* "Marius" V

"It's all a matter of ideas, and God is just one idea I don't accept. It's not important. I am not going out and be immoral or commit crimes because I don't believe in God. I don't even think about it. It's just that I get tired of Him getting credit for all the things the human race achieves through its own stubborn effort. There simply is no blasted God. There is only man, and it is he who makes miracles."

—Beneatha Younger in Lorraine Hansberry's
A Raisin in the Sun, I.i.

"'Tis not enough to help the feeble up
But to support him after."

—*Timon of Athens*, I.i.

"He has taken on the hardest job in any community, which is to mend and heal the broken heart of a child, and he has made it look easy."

—Latricia Tyson, of Mark Slakey, "My English
Professor," *Delta Winds*, Volume 20, edited
by William Agopsowicz and Robert Bini

CHAPTER 1

ALICIA

I see the porky *gringa* with the badass tats on her neck and the filthy overcoat stagger in and slump into a seat in the far corner of the café. *No tip from that one*, I tell myself right away. I hope Clara will take that table herself. I know that sounds mean, but if you've never worked in a restaurant, you have no idea how much it sucks to be stiffed after you've put yourself out there, done your best to be bright and shiny polite, forgetting whatever *mierda* you've been through so far that day to give the customer a big smile and show some interest in lives that led them to our little hole-in-the-wall café in, let us just say, not the finest part of town.

I should be fair. Clara's a good cook, and her food is always tasty. It's just that the kind of customers who come in here tend to bring you down. I'm sure you have seen them: the couples who come in and sit down and their cell phones are out before their bottom even hits the chair. They spend their whole meal texting and checking messages and surfing the Net instead of talking to each other or even looking at each other. Or if their phones aren't right in their faces, the older couples, then one of them, usually the woman, is talking her head off about some stupid show she saw on TV. Her husband is sitting there with this dazed look in his eyes, *Just kill me now*, and when you bring him his plate he practically grabs it out of your hands and starts stuffing in enchiladas like he's spent the last two months marching in a caravan from Caracas. His wife just keeps right on yakking, or maybe she interrupts her fascinating narrative long enough to complain about the food before she's even tasted it, as if instead of the tamale she ordered I served her a turd. The husband finally looks at her and you can tell he's ready to kill *her* now. *Just shut up and eat*, you can see him thinking, and he's probably thinking also about snatching the food off her plate and shoveling that in, too, because his own is gone by now.

You can't help wondering what a stimulating conversation these two must have in the car afterward. He'll be burping up Clara's extra spicy salsa all the way home, while she's giving him a pop quiz on the plot of the TV show to find out how much attention he wasn't paying. Usually the guy is losing his hair or bald already, and his wife is carrying many pounds she really doesn't need. You wonder what either one of them could possibly have seen in the other that caused them to get together in the first place and how they ever had relations and whether they produced any children. If they did, you just hope the kids aren't as hopeless as their parents.

When you see a couple like that, which I'm looking at right now, as a matter of fact, and which I see every time I come to work here, it really makes you question the whole idea of marriage and family. If I'm going to wind up in a marriage like *that*, I'd rather go back to Mexico and join a convent. I'll spend my days praying like Saint Martha, for pigs to fall out of the sky to feed the people in my village. Those are the kinds of thoughts you have when you work at a café like Clara's.

"Then why are you still working there?" Tori is always asking. She works uptown at The Roadhouse and makes a couple hundred bucks in tips on a decent night. All you have to do, she says, is put on a scoop-neck top and make sure to bend down a lot in front of the guys who think they are players. Usually, she says, they are there with their wife and kids, but they still like to take a look, and they are willing to pay for it. I'm lucky to come away with forty or fifty dollars here, on top of the barely more than minimum wage that Clara can pay. But the answer to Tori's question is easy: it's Clara.

To me, Clara Birdsong is America. If you tried to trace her roots on ancestry.com, your computer would probably blow a fuse. She was born on a reservation, and she's part Cherokee. Even she is not sure how much—but it's a lot more than that *rubia* who is running for President, that's for sure. She's also part black, part white, and part Mexican, and she thinks she has a Chinese ancestor somewhere along the line as well. It looks to me as if there is some Egyptian, like Cleopatra, in her, too. Lucky for her, she got the best features of each race. I have seen pictures of her when she was my age or a little more, and she looked just amazing then. She still looks good even though she's really old now, almost sixty. She's the one who hired me, gave me my first job five years ago when I was just fourteen, fresh across the border, and barely spoke enough English to take orders and get them right. She was patient with me, forgave all my screw-ups, even a couple of complete melt-downs when my *pendejo* customers got totally out of control. She never fired me or even threatened to, no matter how much I messed up. She even gives me a little raise each year, nothing Tori wouldn't sneer at, but all Clara can afford from what she squeezes out of the café.

She made her own way in the world. She never even knew her father. He was murdered a month before she was born, and her mother died when she was eight years old. Her father's family tracked her down, moved her off the reservation, and put her to work in the fields when she was ten. She has been taking care of herself and others ever since. She has owned several businesses, and she built the one she has now from the ground up and even rescued it from one of her alcoholic exes, who tried to turn it into a piano bar, if you can imagine that in this part of town, with himself at the keyboard, before *he* got shot and killed in a liquor store parking lot. "If that old *borracho* had tried to play *'Dimé'* one more time before we got rid of that piano, I'd have shot him myself," she says. All this was long before I came along, but I don't doubt it could have happened that way. Clara keeps a gun behind the counter, and I'm sure she's a good shot. She is good at everything really, except men, of course, which makes everything else she's good at sort of irrelevant. If you have to pick one thing to be bad at, men are a really terrible choice. Her first husband gave her two kids and then moved in down the street with her best friend. Her second husband gave her two more and then died in a DUI collision that he caused. Piano man was number three.

The good thing about Clara is she can laugh at her own mistakes, as well as mine. Tori's always talking about asshole bosses who can't wait to chew you out for the slightest slip-up, but Clara has seen enough crazy days go by that she can shake her head and smile when you do something careless or dumb, which I admit I used to do a lot when I was just learning, although now I pride myself on doing a good job and keeping mistakes to a minimum. "Even if you don't make a lot of money, even if no one else notices what you do, do a good job because you are the one doing it. You will know," Papi always used to say—how many times? A million?—when we were together in Mexico. Whenever he laid bricks or put stucco on a new house, the work had to be *perfecto*. I carry his words in my heart even though now we are far apart.

I give up on Clara's taking the table—she's not moving too well any more, and she usually waits for me to make the rounds—and go over to bring the *gringa* a glass of water and a menu. Along the way I have to twist out of reach when Maximo grabs at me. He's an old-timer with no front teeth who always wants a pinch of flesh with his coffee. Basically he's harmless, but I don't let him touch me. "Ugh," I can hear Tori, "how do you put up with that shit? And for a grimy quarter tip?"

I look at the *gringa* over the top of the menu. Up close I almost can't believe how terrible she looks. Her hair is wild and greasy, and her make-up is a mess. Hard to tell what is under that awful overcoat, but I'm sure whatever it is isn't color-coordinated. *How does any woman let herself leave the house looking like that?* Mami drilled into my sisters and me, from the time we were little, the importance of always looking our best when we go out in public. Even when we had next to nothing, she made sure every day to brush our hair and put a ribbon in and to dress us in clean clothes before sending us off to school. You did *not* leave Mami's house without a thorough self-inspection in the mirror, and I still do that every day, before I come to work or school. Between paying for my classes and books and other bills, there's not much left in my budget for clothes or make-up, and I'm always in a rush to get to one place or the other, but at least I take a moment to make sure that I don't look *como algo que el gato trajo de los pelos,* as Mami used to say. Not a Tori moment, of course, which can last an hour and lead to open warfare over whose turn it is in the bathroom.

I know I have some advantages in the looks department, with my complexion (Tori calls it creamy caramel: she says I have the best skin she's ever seen) and my thick, healthy hair. Guys are always telling me how attractive I am, even beautiful many have said, especially, of course, the ones trying to get me into their bed, which is basically all of them. Good luck with that to those *marginados* who dropped out of high school to spend their lives playing video games or working in chop shops. I am going to be a doctor, and I don't need a guy like that holding me back. "Why not be a nurse and marry a doctor instead, honey?" Tori always wants to know. "Let him deal with the stress and the bills for medical school, and you can help him spend his money when he gets out." That's a good plan for her, I guess, but I want my life to be about who *I* am and not just who I'm married to. I've seen what happens to women who depend on men. My sisters back in Mexico have to ask their husbands for money all the time, for every purchase, even to buy groceries or pay a small bill, and they hate it. They always tell me do not put myself in this position.

"Can you get me a straw for this ice water?"

The *gringa* speaks very softly. I can barely hear her, but I nod and lean forward, and I notice again what a mess her hair is. I feel really sorry for girls who have thin hair or greasy hair like this one, although I can't help thinking that shampooing once in a while might help.

"Anything else? You ready to order?"

"Just the straw."

Great. A new low: a trip back to the kitchen just to fetch a *pinche* straw. That's what you get for bringing water to a customer before she orders. Maybe that law against this makes more sense than I gave it credit for. Now they're talking about getting rid of the straws, too. I spin and head for the kitchen, sidestepping Maximo again along the way, then grab a straw and hurry back, only to find the table empty.

Mierda! I wasn't fast enough or what? I practically sprinted to the kitchen and back. I look around and shake my head in disbelief. Maybe Tori is right. Maybe it's time to give up on this job and get a better one. From behind the counter Clara catches my eye and motions toward the restroom. Oh, great. I can only hope the *gringa* isn't spilling her guts in there. With no budget for a janitor, the restroom clean-up tasks fall to me as well. I don't have any time to waste now if I'm going to get to school on time for my class. I head in to see if I can prevent disaster, at least get her to relieve herself in the toilet instead of the sink.

The door is ajar, but I find no *gringa* inside. Instead, I see her discarded overcoat on the floor. I can't believe my eyes.

Swaddled inside it is a tiny new caramel-colored baby.

CHAPTER 2

CLARA

I ain't gonna lie to you: when I hear my girl Alicia yellin' my name, I'm thinkin' maybe that crazy white girl cut her own throat in my restroom. I run in there—well, maybe *run* ain't quite the right word for what I do these days; back in the day, when I was quicker on my feet, I'd have tore after her, chased down that girl, give her a whuppin', beat some sense into her, let her know you drop your baby at the hospital, not on the floor of my café. Anyway, I get in there right quick, considerin', and there's my girl lovin' up that poor child like an angel just fell straight out of heaven into my toilet.

Alicia fixin' to be a baby doctor one day, but she got a lot to learn. She's thinkin' the mama might've cut the cord right in there in and flushed it, but with four of my own childrens and eleven of theirs, I been around enough birthings and such to know this baby girl been in the world at least a few days. Her poor pitiful mama had stuck a pacifier in her mouth, too little for that shit, but she suckin' on it and smilin' up at Alicia like *she* the one brought her into this world. This baby knew a little more about the world she borned into, she might not be smilin' so much. Hard enough bein' borned black in this country—oh, yeah, I could tell right away her daddy's color—and then you add in nobody to take care of you, and a mama that look like she might been on the needle, no tellin' what kind of diseases she might have gave you, you born into a world of hurt.

With Donald Dump doin' everything he can to get rid of Obamacare, we gonna see more and more of this. That man ought to skip his trip to Florida some weekend, swing by here instead, see how all them changes he all day makin' is affectin' folks who don't kiss his butt on the golf course, tell him how great he is, and then go fetch when he knock a putt into the quicksand.

Alicia say, "I'm takin' her home with me. Just for tonight."

"You crazy, girl? Want to get busted and sent back to Mexico? We callin' the cops right now, and—"

"Can't we wait until morning? It's already late. Who knows what kind of care she'll get at this hour. At least I know I can keep her warm and cozy."

Alicia in love with babies. Can't stand yet to let a man who gonna give her one put a hand on her, let alone insert his business, but she got this high and mighty notion 'bout savin' the world's babies.

"You got formula at your house? I don't think so. You got no milk for her in your titties, neither."

"I'll stop at the drugstore on the way home after class, and—"

"What you gonna do when you in class, stick this baby in your backpack?"

"Okay, I'll skip my class tonight, and—"

"What you gonna do when she start bawlin' at three a.m., won't stop for nothin', when you supposed to be gettin' your rest so you can hit them books tomorrow? You even think of that? You fixin' to fall asleep in class? Get your degree, go to medical school like you plannin' to, then you can help plenty of babies."

"The other girls will help me tonight."

Alicia live with three other girls, all of 'em fixin' to be nurses—she the only one bold enough to shoot for doctor. She got Tori, a sister who look a movie star, act like one, too. Martha the white girl whose poor crippled grandma got the house they livin' in. And this year they took in another girl, I can't call her name, she from some awful place in Asia when they still killin' each other just for fun. They all real smart girls, won't none of 'em end up like me still bustin' tail in a diner, but ain't none of 'em ready to take care of a baby just a few days out of her mama's belly.

"Martha's grandma will help us with the baby, too."

Oh, my Lord! That good lady been in a wheelchair since *Jesus* was a baby. She real kind, got a heart for helpin' others, but she need plenty of help herself. "You know she can't be takin' care of no newborn. Neither can you. I'm callin' the police right now."

Alicia get this look in her eye that I never seen before. "If you make that call, I'm quitting my job. Right now. I mean it, Clara. I've never asked you for anything else, but now—"

You never asked me for nothin' else? How 'bout the job I give you when you could barely say your name and what's for supper? "Don't you threaten me, girl."

Now she start to cry. "I'm not threatening you, Clara. I'm begging you. We can't know what kind of treatment she'll get tonight from cops or whoever they turn her over to. Just let me take her home tonight, and first thing tomorrow I'll call and—"

We'll never know whether she would've made that call or how it would've worked out. I won't lie to you: I might've caved and let her take that baby girl home, just for the night. Turns out, though, one of my other customers—not that they was exactly linin' up outside the door—heard the ruckus we was makin' and called the cops on her cell phone.

Two of 'em come in—white man, big fat tomcat, little midget lady, young thing, look like from the Philippines, all business— take a description of the mother, scoop up baby girl, and gone, just like that. Alicia start bawlin' like her heart broke, ain't never gonna heal.

I give her a hug, tell her she still got her job if she want it. Truth is, she a good girl, a hard worker, she don't take nothin' home without askin', and I ain't got time nor inclination to train somebody new.

"Who knows," I tell her, "we check the toilet end of the day tomorrow, maybe we find twins."

CHAPTER 3

OFFICER MASON

You work as a cop in Stockton as long as I have, nothing surprises you anymore. Baby abandoned in a greasy spoon's restroom? Could've been in a garbage can. One time me and my partner found one buck naked in a fucking dumpster. Another one got abandoned near here at night in winter on a highway two hundred feet from a fire station where they would have taken it in, no questions asked. A hitchhiker found that one by sheer accident, or the baby would have died from exposure. Some women just got no business becoming mothers. And you can imagine what a pillar of society this one's baby-daddy must be. The mamas just have shit-for-brains when it comes to who they hit the sheets with. On top of that they're too stupid or too lazy or too passive to make him put a fucking condom on. Ten minutes of pleasure, or a half-an-hour if they're lucky, and then nine months to pay the price. And me and you pay taxes for the rest of our lives to support what they throw away.

You don't like my attitude? You sound just like my partner. She's a newbie, still all charged up to save the world. Give her a few years on the job, a few more meet-and-greets with the Southside Norteños and the Triple Six, she'll come around to my point of view. They all eventually do. She might even quit in a year or two. Lots of the women cops in this town do. Sign up thinking they're gonna restore law and order to Dodge City, find out it's a little tougher than it looks. A badge and a gun don't get the job done.

I used to be just like her, except I was born and raised here. Went to school, played ball, made a million friends—and girlfriends!—of every kind and color. Black, white, or brown, gay, straight, or in-between, man, woman, or can't decide, legal or illegal, I don't care. As long as you behave like a decent human being, you got no problem with me. I joined the force to try to give something back to this place where I grew up. Married a local gal, bought a house two blocks from my parents' house, five minutes from hers, started a family, figured I'd spend the rest of my life right here. Now, though, I'm not so sure. When you see the crap that's happening around here every day when you just go out and try to do your job—the shooters in the streets, this baby being dumped like a sack of shit—it's hard to think about sticking around forever. We got a hotshot young mayor—Stanford man, no less—tryin' to clean this city up, but it's hard to see how he's gonna get it done. No room in the jail to keep the perps more than overnight, fuckhead judges letting the violent offenders back out with a slap on the wrist or a bracelet on their ankle after you risk your life to bring them in. Might as well just hand them the keys to the city. God forbid you fire your piece if you catch them, oh, say, robbing a bank in broad daylight. If a civilian happens to go down, an unlucky bystander, you can kiss your career goodbye.

A few years ago a bunch of our guys got nailed by the media when they gave chase and tried to save a hostage who got carried off. They say *our* guys killed her with their shots, not the scumbags who robbed the bank and abducted her. Everybody in the world thinks they know how to do our job better than we do. I'd like to see what some of those know-it-all journalists would have done if a killer came out of a bank and pointed a hand-cannon in *their* face. I guarantee you they'd throw down their precious notepad or their TV camera and dive under the nearest vehicle, then hide there pissing their panties until a cop came to tell them it's safe to come out and go home. Two of my buddies transferred to the forces in other cities, and two others quit after that fiasco. Working private security now. Shit wages and bennies but at least no pussy reporters to answer to.

Eighty miles west, in San Francisco, they got it even worse. Used to be *The City by the Bay*, the most beautiful burg in the world, some said. Now they got heroin addicts shooting up for breakfast on the sidewalk. You can't even drive there for the day anymore without getting your windshield smashed and your car broke into—after you already got killed on the hit for parking it! Maybe you saw in the news the story about the judge there who keeps kicking loose the car burglar that the cops have caught a dozen times, including several times *in the act* and in possession of weapons. I hope on his next working day that fine, upstanding citizen stumbles across the judge's Jaguar and blows a hole in it with a bazooka, which he can probably pick up cheap on the street no problem these days, God bless the NRA.

I got two more years to get my twenty in. Then, I don't care what the wife says about staying near our families, with or without her I'm gonna think about heading for Oregon or Washington or Idaho, some place a little more civilized. Some place where cops aren't targets for every wannabe looking to make his bones in a gang. Some place where babies are born into families where their mothers actually take care of them. All that blather you hear about *It takes a village to raise a child*? I'll tell you what: if you let the village raise your kids, what you wind up with is a bunch of village idiots. I wouldn't give a Chinaman's chance in Harlem for the future of that little half-breed we just picked up here.

The call wasn't a complete waste of time, though: that waitress who found the baby has a hell of a chassis on her. Wouldn't mind hitting that. If the wife stays on strike and my hot little partner doesn't come across pretty soon, maybe I'll park Santos at the station to write up a report or polish her toenails, then swing by here again solo sometime. See if chiquita's in a better mood to appreciate a man in uniform.

CHAPTER 4

OFFICER SANTOS

Mason is such a tool. We come in here to rescue a helpless infant, and all he can do is drool over the poor girl who found her. I wonder what his wife thinks about all of his extracurricular activities. Ten bucks says he tries to get me to stop in at this café next week so he can check her out again. Or maybe he'll come on his own, off duty. I doubt it, though. He thinks girls are impressed by his uniform, never mind that he's thirty pounds overweight and barely fits into it anymore.

The girl didn't look too impressed to me. Poor thing actually thought she could talk us into leaving the baby with her overnight. As if we can just make up the rules about stuff like that as we go along. People are so ignorant about what police officers can and can't do. I'm just trying to do my job straight up every day. Of course, cops like Mason are breaking the rules all the time, so it's not too hard to figure out why people get confused. I'll bet if that girl had offered to go out with him, he'd have handed that baby over to her without thinking twice—or tried to. Of course, I'd never let him get away with it.

I don't let him get away with anything. I might be only five-foot two, and he might be six-three, like our pussy-grabbing President claims to be, but I let him know right now when he's out of line. He keeps asking *me* to go out with him. Yeah, like that's gonna happen. He and his wife are supposedly *separated.* Separated by what, a phrase? Even if he showed me the legal document, I'd never go out with him. Mixing up that kind of stuff with work—especially this kind of work—is guaranteed to blow up your career before you've barely even begun. They warned me at the Academy about guys like him making moves on new women in the department. Besides, he's not half as hot as he thinks he is. He's always checking himself out in the mirror when he thinks I don't notice. He's way too old for me, though, and too fat, and even if he got in shape, he's hardly my type, anyway. I bet he hasn't read a book since he joined the force. He can't even use proper English. I learned more in grammar school back in the Philippines than he did in high school here. Once I got here, I *hated* my parents for sending me to St. Mary's when all my friends were going to public schools, but when I see the way he struggles to put one word next to another, I'm glad they insisted. I always have to clean up after him when he tries to write a report. Usually, of course, he tries to get me to write it, like I'm his secretary or something instead of his partner.

One time he put his hand on my thigh while I was driving. I stopped so short he almost bashed his head on the windshield. I told him if he ever touches me again while I'm driving, I'll draw on him and shoot his dick off, proving I can hit a small target. And it'll be his turn to write up the report afterward.

The irony is they put him in a car with me to teach me the ropes and keep me safe, but I'm the one who winds up keeping him out of trouble. If he asks me to swing by that café next week, I'll just ask him again how his wife is doing and what they're having for dinner. Or maybe I'll tell him he and his wife should adopt the baby we picked up. That should be good for a big fat laugh. He'd be more interested in adopting a pole-dancer.

I just hope that little one gets adopted into a good home. What happened to her was a pretty rough way to start out your life. I know we couldn't do it, but maybe sending her home with that waitress wouldn't have been such a bad idea after all. I could see the kindness in her eyes. I know, kindness doesn't pay the bills, doesn't put a roof over your head—but it's not a bad place to start.

CHAPTER 5

EDUARDO

Expect the unexpected.

That's one thing the Army definitely beats into you. Some Afghan security guard pretending to be your best friend forever, dreaming of nothing but immigrating to America, land of milk and honey and cable TV, could turn out to be an undercover jihadi in a suicide vest, just waiting for a chance to throw his arms around you and blow you and a barracks-full of your best buddies to Kingdom Come. I knew a few guys who died that way.

I'm on my way to the parking lot after my history class, crossing the bus-stop in front of the campus and thinking about the essay I just got back from Professor Bisson with a grade that made me very happy, when I see this sketchy guy come out of the shadows and go after a girl who is hurrying to catch the bus. The college really cuts corners on lighting, so it's dark and hard to see clearly. At first I think it's just a girlfriend/boyfriend argument, none of my business, but when he catches up with her, grabs her shoulder, and spins her around, I change my mind. I see the confusion, then fear, in the girl's eyes. My training kicks in, and I step up. In a few quick strides I'm right in his kitchen.

"Is there a problem here?" I say to her. "Anything I can do to help?"

He answers me instead. "Fuck off, faggot."

I unshoulder my backpack, just in case, as I take another step toward him. I smell the weed on him now. I've been known to indulge myself, of course—who doesn't? It's even legal now—but this guy reeks of it. As I get closer, he lets go of the girl and pulls a knife out of a pocket.

"You want some of this, motherfucker?"

I always wonder how guys who think they are badasses decide that they can take on someone else. Someone like me, for instance. I'm not a huge guy, and I'm not cut like I was when I was deployed, but I don't think anyone with any sense would look at me and think *There's a punk-ass I can make my bitch*, which is more or less what he says to me next. Of course, he has no way of knowing that he's coming at someone who spent four years in the Rangers, with two tours of Afghanistan. Before that I wrestled for four years in high school. Won league and section my senior year and made it to state. Got my ass kicked there, but not by some skinny pothead in dreads, practically tripping over his own pants. It's pretty clear that only one of us has exchanged fire with the Taliban and walked away alive. His combat experience is probably more along the lines of bullying the pre-teen lookouts on the block he grew up on. If some recruiter humping to meet his quota ever signed this guy up, I see him washing out of boot camp in the first five minutes. He wouldn't last five seconds at Fort Benning, that's for sure. Still, he has a knife.

Try to defuse.

I give him a chance to reconsider his options here. "Put the knife on the ground and walk away."

Instead he lunges at me. With my left hand I swing my backpack to block the knife, then with my right I deliver a short, hard chop, just like we were taught, to his wrist, which quite possibly breaks. He howls and drops the knife, which falls to the ground. Then he tries to kick me in the balls. I skip back quickly out of range, catch his leg on the uplift with my hand, then flip him up and over, high and hard. His head hits the concrete with a thump that says maybe a concussion. I draw my own foot back to kick *him* in the balls, show him how it's done—what can I say? It seems like a teachable moment—when the girl grabs my arm and yells at me not to do it.

The guy is down for a bit, definitely no threat for the moment, so I take the time to check the chick out. She's Mexican, like me, or Hispanic anyway, and it suddenly hits me that she's also drop-dead gorgeous. It's not like me to lose track of a detail like that, trust me, but under the circumstances you can understand that I was a little distracted. I see a thousand beautiful faces on this campus every day, but this is maybe the most beautiful girl I've ever seen.

I lean down to pick up the punk's knife, which is about as impressive as his vocabulary. It looks like he got it on sale at The Dollar Store. Even a cheap knife can kill you, though. It's filthy, and you could die from sepsis even if the wound it gave you was superficial. It would really suck, after surviving an IED in Ghazni, to get taken out by a homegrown goon who can't even keep his weapon clean.

I hold the blade up for her inspection. She doesn't seem to know what to make of it, but she doesn't seem too freaked out, either. I realize that she never panicked or screamed, even in that first moment of fear. Given what has just gone down, I'm impressed with how calm she is.

The guy on the ground groans, tries to raise his head. I put my foot on his sternum. Then I realize I've seen this guy before. After another evening class a month or so ago, I came out to the parking lot and found him jiggling the handle of the passenger-side door on my car. He was eyeing the glove box, where I occasionally store some pretty good shit.

"Nice ride you've got there."

"Fuck off, motherfucker. This shit ain't mine."

"I know. It's mine."

"No crime in takin' a look."

He'd moved on quickly that time, maybe missing his *ganga* courage, or maybe just in search of a softer target. I probably should have called the cops on him then, but chances are it would have turned into a *your word against his* kind of deal, with a cop, probably white, choosing not to get involved in a brown-versus-black dispute. This time, though, I had his knife and a witness, nearly a victim.

He groans again. I step on him a little harder.

"You got a cell phone?" I ask her.

"Of course."

"Want to call this in for me? Wait, I've got a better idea."

I tell him to turn over, face down on the ground. He tries to resist this, but I slide my foot up to his Adam's apple, and he gets the message and turns over. I pull his cell phone—another cheap piece of shit, which he probably lifted from a six-year-old—out of his back pocket, down around the middle of his thighs, and hand it to her.

"Dial 9-1-1."

She frowns for a second, like she doesn't quite understand.

"This way the cops will have his number. Make it more convenient for them next time they need to get in touch."

She dials but hands the phone back to me. I quickly explain what's going on and where we are. The campus cops get a redirect call and show up within a couple of minutes. They've seen this guy before, probably busted him, too. He might even be a student here, or more likely a drop-out. The girl doesn't say much, mostly just shakes her head at their questions. One of them sees my Ranger tat, gives me a nod. They cuff the punk and get ready to take him away. He'll probably be out and back in action within twenty-four hours, poster child for the school-to-prison pipeline.

"You got somethin' of mine," he yells, as the cops stuff him into the back of their SUV.

"Was he talking to you or to me?" I ask her.

"Must be you. I've never seen him before tonight."

I nod. "I have." I tell her about interrupting his attempt

to break into my car. "Maybe he thinks I hung onto his shitty knife." Of course I had turned it over to the cops. "But it looked like he was maybe following you."

"I think I did see him earlier at the bus stop near the restaurant where I work, before I came to class. Maybe he was after my tips? He wouldn't have gotten much."

The restaurant where she works. I'll have to find out where that is.

"Thank you," she finally says, which I've been wondering if I was ever going to hear from her. Again, I make allowances for the circumstances. She was a bit distracted, too. "I've got some protection in my purse, but I don't know if I would have been able to get it out in time to use it."

She turns to go.

"I'm Eduardo," I blurt, before she can get out of hearing range. I rack my brain for something brilliant to say before she slips away and I never see her again in my life.

Here's what I come up with, in case you want to write it down for future use: "Want to get a cup of coffee?"

CHAPTER 6

ALICIA

I can't *believe* I gave him my phone number. I *never* do that with a guy I just met. I never do that with any guy, really. Even as he is putting the number into his phone, I'm thinking what Mami would say: have you gone *loco*? He could be a mental patient who will knock on your door at 3:00 a.m. to bring you a chicken. He could be a stalker who will wait for you outside of every classroom door, or follow you to work and get you fired. He could be a serial killer! He has been in the Army, so he knows all about guns. Maybe you just gave your phone number to the next mass murderer. Mami watches a lot of news from America on TV.

I tell myself to stay calm. I remind myself that this guy— Eduardo Martinez, I really like his name—has just rescued me from someone else who may actually fit one of Mami's descriptions.

It was just such a crazy way to meet someone! One minute I'm rushing to catch the bus and thinking what to do about the baby, and the next I'm in the middle of an episode of *Lockup*. The other girls at school and in my house are always talking about all the crime on campus. Many have had their purses or backpacks stolen or their cars broken into, but it never happened to me before. Of course, I don't have a car to be broken into, so I guess that is lucky for me, but I am as much of a target as the next woman when I am walking by myself. Papi taught all of his daughters how to defend ourselves, and I always figure I can handle myself in any situation, but I wonder how much good my little can of pepper spray would have done—if I even had time to get it out and didn't shoot it off in my own face instead of his, like Martha did to herself when she was trying to show me how to use it. I guess it's a good thing Eduardo was there to help me.

I'll bet even Tori would be impressed by this guy. He's really cute—I like it that he keeps his hair short and neat, not like that bedhead bird's-nest you see on so many guys at school—and *órale*, those muscles! I guess in the Army they really get you in shape. He certainly knew how to handle that attack. I wonder what he would have done to that guy if I had not been there to stop him. Maybe I even kept him out of some trouble he might have got himself into by going too far. I'm glad he listened to me and stopped.

I have to admit, he makes a great first impression. He isn't pushy about getting coffee, just lets it go when I tell him waiting for the cops has made me late for my bus. He offers to drive me home, but I tell him I would rather just wait for the next bus. So he waits here with me. He tells me a little bit about himself. It doesn't seem like he really wants to talk too much about being in the Army, though. Mostly we talk about school. What a coincidence that he wants to be in the medical field, like me. I wonder if we'll have any classes together. It still seems kind of strange to me that men want to be nurses now: they get first crack at all the other decent jobs, so maybe they should just leave nursing to us women! When I tell him I want to be not a nurse but a doctor, I'm half-expecting him to laugh in my face like others have done, or ask me how in the world I'm going to pay for medical school. Instead, he just smiles and nods and says that he admires me for aiming high.

When I tell him about finding the baby, he seems interested. He doesn't laugh at me, either, for wanting to keep her. He just listens and then says that he hopes I will be successful. It shows he's not one of those jerks who thinks only about himself all the time. The Tori Collection, in other words.

"Thanks for giving me your number," he says, with another smile, as the next bus pulls up. "You'll have mine when I call."

We'll see about that. Tori says guys always take your number, but they never follow through after they promise to call. If they don't call *her*, what chance do I have? I'll probably never see him again—but I am glad that he was here tonight.

CHAPTER 7

TORI

"You seriously were going to bring a baby home with you?"

"I hadn't really thought it through. It just seemed like the right thing to do. Those cops who came—they just seemed so cold."

"They're cops. What do you expect?"

"I don't know. I *didn't* expect to find a baby on the restroom floor."

"In a damn overcoat, you say?"

Alicia nodded. "All she could give to her own baby."

"Now you gettin' sentimental on me. She better off keep her legs crossed, you ask me."

"Be an immaculate virgin like you, you mean?"

"Watch your lip or I'll kick your ass."

"Sorry. It just seemed a little hypocritical."

"That's my business, not yours. Tell me more about this Latin Batman who came to your rescue."

"Not much more to tell."

"Did you at least give him your phone number?"

She smiles, and I know she did.

"Don't count on him callin', though."

"I know. How'd it go for you tonight with God's Gift to Womankind?"

Alicia got a little thing for my Henry herself, I can tell. Can't hardly blame her for that. He is one gorgeous hunk of man. Kind of like Cam Newton's face on top of LeBron's body, if you know what I mean, and if you don't get the picture I'm paintin', you spendin' too much time on the damn shopping channel and neglectin' your NFL and NBA. But Alicia know I saw him first, and she fair about shit like that. Besides, Henry already dropped out of the class we met him in. He ain't much for hittin' the books, and Alicia plannin' on a double bookworm wedding. Plannin' to be a doctor and marry one, too, you imagine that?

Now I got to update her on the Henry situation. We been eyeballin' each other for a while, but this the first time I was actually supposed to go out with him.

"Let me ask you somethin': did you know that the average American adult male has a more intense emotional relationship with his car or his truck than with his wife or his girlfriend?"

"Where did you hear that? In your Marriage and Family class?"

"Nope. Read it in *Cosmo*."

"Well, then, it *must* be true."

"Just think about it, girl: all these guys you see spending hours every weekend detailing their vehicle, washing and polishing and spit-shinin' it to make it look just perfect. Same guys can't be bothered to take five minutes helpin' out inside with the housework or playin' with their kids, but they got all these hours for their ride. It's like their whole life revolves around what they drive."

"So is that the problem with Henry?"

"I wish. He got the opposite problem."

"What do you mean?"

"When was the last time you saw a black man drivin' a Pinto?"

"I don't really pay too much attention to cars."

"All you got to know about this one is they stopped makin' 'em forty years ago."

"Oh. It's a classic, then."

"It's a piece of shit. He say he enjoy the challenge of fixin' it up and keepin' it runnin'. I say back I hope he enjoy just as much the challenge of gettin' a second date with me, 'cause the first one just ended."

"You really refused to go out with him just because of the car he drives?"

"Damn straight. I ain't gettin' my ass into no Ford Pinto. Word gets out about me doin' that, next thing you know I'll have dudes tryin' to pick me up on a scooter."

She laughs at that. Got to keep your sense of humor when it come to dealin' with the primates.

"Guess I gotta make me a new first date rule: make sure to ask up front about what he fixin' to chauffeur me in. All these men givin' all this love to their rims and their rides, and I wind up with Pinto Bro."

"What about that manager at the restaurant who's been hitting on you? You said he drives a BMW, didn't you?"

"Andrew? Shit, that fool on me again last night, tryin' to paw me before I even get my time-card punched in, pretendin' to be mad 'cause I'm five or ten minutes late. Don't even hardly give me room to turn around and tell him to his face he need to suck on a breath mint. He just a office slave anyway. Manager at a damn chain restaurant, makin' fifty, maybe sixty thousand a year, if he lucky. Most of that go to payments and insurance on his Bimmer, I imagine. I tell him to get back to me when he *own* a franchise, maybe then we got somethin' to talk about."

"I hope he got your message."

"Hell, no. Just wait: he be right back on top of me next shift. So what you gonna do about this damn baby you fell in love with?"

She say Moua maybe got a plan to help out with that. This I gotta see. That bitch more likely to eat a baby than love it up, you ask me.

CHAPTER 8

MOUA

So on the bus on the way to our classes in the morning, I fill Alicia in on my brainstorm to help her track down the little bundle of trouble she found in the crapper last night. It's the least I can do, really; after all, Alicia is the one who persuaded Martha and the g-ma to take me in. I'm sure they would have preferred to rent the last bedroom to another hardcore Christian. To tell you the truth, I needed that room so bad that I was almost ready to fake it, baptize myself with a can of Sprite or something and be Born Again, just to get the great rate they were asking.

The reason I needed the room so bad was to keep me from hanging myself in a closet or strangling my mom in her sleep. I just couldn't live under her roof another minute. She was on me like 24/7, trying to keep me off social media—which is practically the only life I have—and throwing a fit if I even got like one A- on a stupid quiz that barely even counted toward the final grade in a class. I kept trying to tell her that the semester grades are the only ones that matter, the only ones that go on your transcript. She just didn't get it, though, and she wouldn't let up. The sick part is she never even graduated from high school herself and never learned how to speak English in a way that anyone outside our family can understand. The way she still talks, she might as well have just stepped out of a pigpen back in Cambodia, or a pew in the g-ma's church when they're feeling the spirit and speaking in tongues. Nobody who isn't kin has a clue what she's trying to say. Up until the day I took off, I was still getting dragged to the bank or the store to translate for her. My kid sister, runt of the litter, got stuck with that wonderful job when I left. She's texting me like every day to beg me to come back. *Mom is driving me f…ing nuts*, the last one said. *I'm going to hire a hit man if you don't come home to help me soon.*

So here's a story: my mom in a nutshell. When I was six years old, I got sent home from first grade after I showed up for my class with the flu and a really bad cough. Mom tells me to go back the next day. Same thing happens. I get sent home again. She tells me how much worse she had it as a kid, when she got the chicken pox, and the soldiers in her village stuck her in a chicken coop and laughed at her, called her names, and spat on her when they passed by. She claims she didn't even cry when they did all that to her. She says I'm just being a baby, and I need to stay in school, or I'll wind up illiterate like her. I tell her I'm not the one sending me home. She smacks me then, and *I* start to cry. She smacks me harder and tells me never to talk back to her again, or she'll give me something to really cry about. She means it, too. She used to hit my brothers with a paddle that had a nail poking through it. Not a tack, a nail. She also has a chicken coop of her own in back of the house, and I wouldn't put it past her to lock me in there and let me duke it out with the roosters.

So next day I go to school again and throw up on the poor kid sitting next to me, and then I actually have some kind of a seizure and pass out on the classroom floor. A nurse comes and takes one look at me, then calls an ambulance and gets me to the hospital. The doctor tells me later I had a fever of 107 degrees. I would have died or at least fried my brain for good if the nurse at the school hadn't stepped in to do what my mom was too stupid or too stubborn to do.

Nobody can tell her anything. She's an absolute despot, her way or the hell way. She puts food on the table and a roof over our heads and in return expects absolute obedience to her rules, no matter how insane or life-threatening they may be. For the next twelve years nothing really changes, except that one by one my seven older siblings escape as soon as they can, leaving the rest of us to fend for ourselves. One of my sisters is so desperate that she marries at age sixteen, just a year older than my mother was when *she* got spliced. This is like five years ago. Ever since, the guy my sister married sends her out to work six days a week at a Taco Bell while he sleeps in, smokes dope all day, and then stays out all night gambling with his homeboys. He loses most of the money that she earns. She says it still beats living at home with mom.

So you can see why I couldn't let this room get away from me, which it would have if Alicia hadn't jumped in and talked me up. It probably didn't hurt my chances that I'm no beauty queen. Neither is Martha, and she probably gets tired of looking at perfect all the time. Tori could pass for Beyoncé's hotter little sister, and Alicia is JLo thirty years ago, only with a brain instead of just a butt. There's no point in being jealous of them: they didn't have anything to do with the equipment they were born with, and it's not their fault if men are practically shooting in their shorts whenever they see them, although Tori doesn't exactly keep them guessing with those tops and thongs she struts around in. I guess you can't really hold it against them. I never yet met a pretty girl who would rather be ugly. Some good-looking girls, though not these two, go out of their way to avoid looking good, but I'll bet it's a temporary mood-swing thing, and girls like that are secretly glad they can flip the switch and go back to gorgeous whenever they feel like it.

There's no switch to flip for Martha and me. I'm not exactly hideous, and neither is she, but let's just say we won't be winning any swimming suit competitions anytime soon. I weigh like ninety-five pounds, and Martha has the opposite problem. When she was running around like a wild child for years, she was almost as skinny as I am, I've seen the pictures, but since she gave up her other addictions, she pounds the carbs a little harder than she probably should. She's not obese or anything, but heavy enough to be self-conscious about it, especially under the same roof with those two goddesses. Men don't slobber over us the way they do over Tori and Alicia, and that's just fine with me. Martha pretends it's fine with her, too, but I think she really wants to get married and start popping out babies instead of finishing school and becoming a nurse.

I don't know how she expects to get into the program anyway. If you're going to be a nurse these days, let alone a doctor, you practically have to have all A's. The nursing major at every university in the state is impacted, and at the community college we go to, there are like five thousand students every year saying they want to get into this field—and fifty or sixty slots, total. It's crazy odds just to get into the program. You'd think we were going to come out of it with a license to mint our own cryptocurrency instead of the training to drain boils and rinse bedsores. Martha got a C in English 1A, and the program basically says you have to get an A in that course to even be considered. I mean, let's face it, if you get a C in that course, the way they hand out grades around here, you might as well have *Too Stupid To Live* tattooed on your forehead. Plus she's taking the lowest level math class for like the third time this semester, and she's never come close to passing it yet. She can't really even do basic arithmetic. I try my best to help her, but it's like trying to teach a frying pan not to burn the eggs. She'd never admit it, but if the right guy came along, I'll bet she'd be happy to quit school, move right out of the g-ma's house, and leave her care to the rest of us.

It does get old, pushing the g-ma around in her wheelchair all day and helping her on and off the hopper. She can't even wipe herself, or at least she won't even try. Whenever I complain, Alicia just says it's good training for what we're in for. She says if you don't enjoy taking care of old people who can't take care of themselves, you've got no business trying to be a nurse, or a doctor like she wants to be. Tori complains about it even more than I do. Alicia doesn't complain about anything, even the nickel more than minimum wage that crazy old Clara pays her at the café where she works.

Alicia's too loyal to Clara to take Tori's advice and put on the Roadhouse uniform. She's got all these lofty ideals about what a woman should or shouldn't do to make it in this world. Personally, I don't have any illusions about that stuff. I come from a long line of comfort women. They never called themselves that, but that's what they were. My mother was basically kidnapped by my father when she was fifteen, even though they were already here in the U.S. by then. That's still the custom back home, and a lot of people from the old country are really big on keeping up their traditions, no matter how nutso: when a guy finds the girl he wants, he just goes and snatches her, and then the two families negotiate a bride-price afterward. My mom's price was fourteen goats. The terms of the transactions vary from one place to another, obviously, but let's face it: for most of history, women have been tools for the needs and pleasures of men. Case in point: my dad. After my kid sister was born, my mom finally got her tubes tied. My dad showed his support for this decision by booking the next flight to Cambodia to bring back another child bride and start a new family. We've never met his new wife or seen him since he took off, but we heard through the grapevine that we have something like six new half-siblings at last count. Mom has devoted the spare time she gained from not having to clean up his messes to punishing the rest of us for his betrayal. Finding a man who *doesn't* treat you like a tool—now there's the quest of a lifetime.

As idealistic as she is, Alicia isn't one hundred percent angel. Her motive for helping me get the room in the g-ma's house wasn't exactly altruistic. When we were in the same math class, she saw my score on the first test that came back, a 98%, when she got like a 76%, and she figured I could help her ace that class. She's no dummy, don't get me wrong just because she needed my help. Unlike Martha, she picked up the stuff I showed her right away, and she wound up with the third highest total score in the class, behind only me and this brainiac from Pakistan who supposedly didn't get a single problem wrong all semester. Alicia told me she used to kick ass in math and science back in Mexico, but when she came here at like fourteen she got stuck in a really messed up high school. She said her teacher for Algebra was some reject from the P. E. Department who used to make these obvious mistakes on the blackboard all the time. When students tried to correct him, he'd tell them to shut up or he'd make them run laps. With dopes like that teaching her, you can't blame her for deciding to let the math and science slide and concentrate on improving her English, which I admit she has done an amazing job of, considering she's only been here for five years—especially compared to my mom, who's been here for *thirty*-five years. Alicia still leaves out a pronoun once in a while or mixes in some Spanish when she can't think of the English, but otherwise you'd hardly know she wasn't born here.

As impressed as I am with her English, she's even more impressed with my math and science. People like her always seem to think that us Asians are born with giant brains and that school is a piece of cake for us. That's about as accurate as thinking all black people can dunk a basketball when they're born, or pick up a saxophone and play every note perfectly without a single lesson. The truth is, school is just as boring for us as it is for everybody else. When some stupid history teacher like the one I have now is rattling on about Hitler's hemorrhoids or some equally inspiring topic, I tune out just as fast as everyone else. I will admit that math and science are easier for me than they seem to be for other people, especially poor Martha, of course, but the only reason I'm good at that stuff is I was really lucky to get a great teacher in high school.

My mom found out about Mr. Vang—everyone just calls him Mr. V—from the parents of some of the other kids who'd had him. She made sure that I took all my math classes from him, and if you can do math, that helps a lot with science. Most of the teachers at the high school, the last bell rings and they're sprinting for the parking lot like the school's on fire and there's a shooter inside, but Mr. V's the kind of guy who will stay after classes as long as you can stay, to make sure that you understand everything in the lesson he's covering. I wouldn't be surprised if he even makes house calls. He's like completely dedicated to his job. He *loves* math. I can't really imagine that: I mean, people love all kinds of crazy stuff—cats, rap, baseball, *Game of Thrones*, Pokémon Go—but to love math in the way he does just seems really hard to fathom.

Unlike most teachers, he doesn't spend a lot of time blabbing about himself, but one day I learned a little more about him. My mom made me stay late to tell him about this scholarship offer I got from CSU and thank him for helping me to get it, even though she wouldn't let me accept it because it was "too far from house"—like Sacramento was in the middle of Africa or something instead of forty-five minutes away. Anyway, I was probably complaining to him about her a little bit, as usual. He took out his wallet and showed me a photo of *his* mother. Turns out it's the only picture of her that he has. When he was six years old, the same Khmer Rouge humanitarians who put my mom in that cage as a kid caught up with *his* mom and arrested her. He was right there watching the whole thing happen when they chopped her head with an axe and dropped her into a ditch. She died in the ditch with a bunch of other people that day. They were killed because they had gone to school for a few years.

I guess it just made Mr. V value his own education all the more when he got the chance. Now he has two master's degrees, and he's won the Teacher of the Year award at the high school like five times in a row. He helps everyone, too, not just the ones whose families came from Cambodia, like me. I know there is still a ton of prejudice here, you'd have to be an idiot not to notice, and I've experienced my share first-hand: *cambo, gook, oriento*, I've been called, and even *chink*. It really sucks when other kids are trying to insult you and they can't even get your ethnicity right. But I have to say that Mr. V's story proves one thing: in this country, as messed up as it may be with DT in the White House, if you are good at your job, you have a chance to be recognized and rewarded for it. As long as DT doesn't deport you, of course.

Anyway, long story short, Alicia was happy when I told her last night I'd help her find the baby. I figured it couldn't be that hard if you knew how to turn on a computer and put Google on the case. I threw in a few phone calls to the police station and the county hospital. I pretended to be a friend of the abandoning mother's, and the cops got real interested for a second, so I had to tone that down a bit. Then this morning I get the bright idea of how to track down the real mother ourselves. Maybe she will let Alicia raise the baby, which for some completely insane reason she has convinced herself she wants to do, on top of going to school full-time and working full-time at Clara's café.

I say to Alicia on the bus now, "What if we offered a reward? Maybe somebody out there knows who she is and will rat her out. Or maybe she's desperate enough to turn herself in."

"Great idea—but where would we get the money to put up the reward?"

"I was thinking more along the lines of an imaginary reward."

"What are you talking about?"

"We offer it, she or someone she knows claims it, and then we explain that we were just bluffing, but we won't turn her in if she ID's the baby as hers and signs something to let us—let you, I mean, I haven't gone completely nuts—raise her."

"Isn't that blackmail?"

"Of course it is. How do you think anything ever gets done in the world? How do you think we wound up with the President that we have? Nobody does anything for nothing. Everything is for sale."

"Maybe you should be majoring in Business Administration instead of Nursing."

"Maybe I should. When they put in a concentration on phone sex, I'm in."

"You're not really doing that, are you?"

"How do you think I paid my rent last month? Don't tell Martha, though. She thinks I'm swapping stocks."

CHAPTER 9

MARTHA

It seems that this baby I've never even seen has become the center of our whole world here in Grandma Vi's house. Sort of like another baby became the center of the world two thousand years ago. I know some people will make fun of me for saying that, just like they make fun of me for everything else I say, I'm just the stupid Bible girl who believes in the good things in this world and a better life ahead in the next one for all of us who accept Jesus. Is it so awful to be an optimist, to have some faith? I don't think so. You wouldn't either if you'd been through what I've been through before I was saved.

Alicia was really hard on the baby's mother, but I don't judge her. How can we know what *she* has been through or what led her to drop that baby off like that? Alicia says she looked like she does drugs. Well, guess what: she's not the only one. I've done drugs, in fact, before I was saved, I did a lot of drugs. Half of the kids at the schools I went to did drugs, some of them even did heroin. I've never done that, but I've tried just about everything else. My first LSD trip, I took my panties off and put them in a mailbox, in the middle of the afternoon. There's even pictures. The so-called friends I was partying with took photos with their cell phones and posted them on Facebook. I forgive them, now, of course, they were just kids. They never thought about how pictures like that could follow me through life and mess up my chances for getting a job later. They were just having fun, making fun of me.

What I don't get is why everybody is so mean to each other all the time. All these rappers everyone loves to listen to with their *motherfucker* this and their *cocksucker* that and their *niggers* and their *bitches* and their *ho's*—what are they contributing with all of their curse words? Why do they have to put everyone else down all the time? Why can't they try to focus on something more positive for a change?

It's like all these people criticizing our President. I know he's not perfect, he's made some mistakes. Grandma Vi says men have urges they can't control, and we have to forgive them. She says there are studies that show men think about sex every seven seconds or so, which is way more often than women do—it sure is way more often than *I* think about it! She even says there were times when Grandpa Jack sort of forced himself on her even though she wasn't in the mood. Tori says there's no such thing as *sort of*, he either forced himself on her or he didn't, except she doesn't say *forced*, she says, "Either he raped you or he didn't." I guess it's hard to know what really happened between two other people when no one else is watching.

Anyway, I sort of wish all these women who are complaining about the President and saying he did all this awful stuff to them in the past would just shut up and let him do his job now. What's wrong with trying to make America great again? We're turning into a country where you can't even take a walk around your own neighborhood without stepping into piles of poop on the sidewalks because the neighbors are too lazy to train their dogs to go in their own backyard or to clean up after them when they don't. This used to be a nice neighborhood, I spent a lot of time here when I was a kid, after my dad took off and my mom got on the pills and spent the whole day sleeping and then stayed up all night drinking wine and watching infomercials on television until Grandma Vi kicked her out. Then of course they had the big fight over who got custody of me, I wound up staying with Grandma Vi for a few years until I ran away. There was no poop on the sidewalks back then, or at least I don't remember any, it was actually a really nice place to live, and I was in a decent school, except for the drugs, I guess. I even had some friends, or sort of friends anyway, but it was just too hard not knowing what was going on with my mom, so I took off and tried to find her. I never did.

I tried to find my dad, too, even though I knew he really didn't care about me. Grandma Vi says he was too young and too selfish to be a father, mom never should have hooked up with him. I still miss him, though. I remember when he used to take me to Lodi and buy me a root beer float at A&W, I thought that was the greatest thing in the world. Sometimes he ate the ice cream and drank most of the root beer himself, but I was happy just to be with him and to have a treat to share. I didn't care that he took most of it, I guess that's just the way men are.

After I ran away, I couldn't find my mom or my dad. I heard later that my dad went to jail for a while, and my mom moved to New Mexico with a guy she used to get her drugs from, we don't know where she is now or even if she's still alive. I started doing drugs myself and hanging out with the kind of people who take pictures of you when you're buzzed and half-naked and post them on social media. It was actually somebody who saw me on Facebook and told Grandma Vi about it that led her to hire a private investigator to track me down and bring me home, that's when she said I could either come to church with her and clean up my act or go back out on the street. I decided to give church a try. Best decision I ever made in my life. Grandma Vi saved me—she and Pastor Greg. He's the one who told me no matter what terrible things I had done in the past, if I put myself in his hands and accepted Jesus as my savior now, I could be forgiven and start a new life. Now I'm studying to be a nurse, so I can help other people every day, I even teach Sunday school and try to help other kids stay out of the kind of trouble I got myself into. It was a lot more than just drugs, believe me.

That's why I don't judge that baby's mother. I hope Alicia can find the baby *and* the mother, maybe we can save both of them. It would be so cool to watch Pastor Greg dedicate that baby. Maybe her mother can be baptized during the same service. Why not? If I could be saved, why not her?

And I hope you won't think I'm too pushy now, but I have to ask, it's my Christian duty: and why not *you*, too?

CHAPTER 10

JACK

So now the little tramp is talking about bringing home a baby to take care of. And not just any baby, either—a crack baby! The miracle is it isn't her own, the way she's been putting herself out on the street since she turned thirteen. Now all of a sudden she's found God like her crackpot grandma—and going to college!

College: what bullshit! A bunch of so-called institutions of higher learning rounding up the biggest thugs they can find on the streets and paying them peanuts to play football or basketball for the school while they pretend to be students. Might as well go straight back to slavery days and watch the plantation owners pit their prize niggers against each other in the mud. Who the fuck do they think they're kidding? It's got nothing to do with education. It's all about the money. Damn football coaches and college presidents making six million a year, taking vacations in Paris and Rome, while an honest working stiff like me that fought for his country can't even find a decent job or take a day off with pay if by some miracle I do.

I tell you, a white man in this godforsaken ghetto town might as well try to swim to Kansas as get a good-paying government job. You go down to the post office to find out why your mail keeps getting delivered to the raghead who lives next door, nobody has any answers for you, and they can't even speak English you can understand half of if they do. Same bullshit when you go down to the damn DMV to try to get your license renewed before you and it expire. I guarantee you'll see every color in the fucking rainbow behind the counters there except white. And then you're gonna stand on your head in line for two hours waiting for some shit-colored fuck-up to find the right form and process it, a job you could train a backward chimpanzee to do in two minutes.

Affirmative Action, they call it, to make up for *white privilege* and *the injustices of the past.* White privilege my ass. The only such bullshit I ever had is I was privileged to see the whites of the eyes of the gooks who came hauling ass out of the bushes to try to gut me with their bayonets when they ran out of bullets. If you ain't seen that for yourself, up close and personal like I did for three tours, don't try to tell me about all the advantages I took for granted. Save your liberal bullshit for someone who might be stupid enough to believe it. That crap's about as convincing as all this Holy Bible mumbo jumbo Vi has pushed on Martha and everybody else who will listen to her babble about the Good Lord who blessed her into that goddam wheelchair.

I stopped listening to her years ago. Some people say I'm lucky my ex let me come back here after goddam PG&E burned down my place in Paradise, especially considering she blames me for running off our own children and ruining their lives. I say shit to that: our kids made their own messes. Who paid for this house they grew up in and lived in free of charge and all the food they ate and all the other shit my paycheck went for, with never so much as a *Thank you, Daddy,* and barely enough left over to buy myself a pack of fucking cigarettes? This same house that Vi is sharing now with her collection of *college girls*: one that's illegal for sure, another that might as well be, and one more that goes around dressed like a whore? Who put twenty years of his life into mortgage payments on this goddam International House of Headcases and wound up living in the garage?

Don't worry, though: it's not like I can't handle it. There's a park across the street with a toilet I can use when I need to drop a log, and there's a faucet outside here I can hook up to a hose with a nozzle so I can take a hobo shower. I've made do with worse. Much worse, actually. If you've ever tried to take a shit or a shower with a bunch of gook bastards shooting at you or trying to carve out your intestines, you know what I mean. If you haven't, it's thanks to guys like me who have.

Just don't try to lecture me about how grateful I should be to God or Vi or anybody else if I get *blessed* to be great-grandpa to some nigger's crack baby dropped off in a toilet stall. Now there's a *white privilege* if I ever heard one! I just hope Miss *I Found Jesus* don't plan to squeeze no baby-sitting duty out of me. Change diapers again at this stage of my life? Shit, I'd rather go back to Vietnam.

CHAPTER 11

EDUARDO

Most girls you meet just want to talk about themselves. Oh, they'll ask a few questions and pretend to listen when you try to tell them what it was like to wake up every morning with terrorists trying to capture you and hack off your head on the World Wide Web, but really they're just waiting for a chance to tell you more about themselves and how crappy their lives are and how unfair it is that they're not rich and famous yet, like Kylie Jenner. This girl is different, though. I can tell right away.

She seems surprised and a little guarded when I phone her the next day. We meet again two nights later at the Starbucks across the street from the campus, half-an-hour before we each have a class. Obviously she has built in an escape hatch in case I come across the wrong way. I'm okay with that and ready to take it slow if that turns out to be the way to go. Sometimes the safety valve is a good option for me, too, if the girl turns out to be a pain-in-the ass who wants to take up our whole first date by telling me the story of her life. But this one asks about me before I can ask about her.

When I tell her a little bit about Afghanistan, she seems really interested. She doesn't just blow it off when I tell her about the brothers I lost over there. She asks me if it was worth it, going halfway around the world to fight in a war that most people here at home don't even care about any more, if they ever did in the first place. It's a long time since 9/11. She was just a baby in Mexico when that happened, and I wasn't much older myself, so it's not surprising that she would ask. I have asked myself the same question many times. I try to be honest with her. I tell her

I enlisted because I wanted to make a difference, to be a part of history, not just someone who sat on the sidelines and watched or worried or tweeted while others put their lives on the line for our country.

"You sound like you miss it," she says, and I realize that she has really been paying attention.

"I miss some things," I tell her. "I don't miss the weather. We hit 120 degrees a few times in summer, hotter than the worst August day I ever spent in Stockton—or in Georgia—and down to 15 degrees in the winter, when you think your toes are going to freeze and break off. I don't miss the food, or the coffee—please, never let your lips touch Army coffee—or some of the training we had to do. We wasted a lot of time doing stupid stuff. But I guess that's true of just about every job. What I do miss is the camaraderie, the sense of purpose that we had. There's something special about knowing that the guys you're serving with have your back no matter what, that they're willing to lay down their life for you. You don't get that feeling as a civilian, at least I don't. Here at school, most of the students seem to be phoning it in, doing just enough to get by. Can't even be bothered to keep up with the reading that the professors assign—and then complain if the quiz or the test is too hard. Of course, that was me in high school, too, so I guess I shouldn't be so hard on everybody else now."

She asks how I got the scars on my arms and my neck. I tell her about hitting the IED in the Humvee I was riding in. She really listens, too, when I tell her about the medics who pulled me out and treated me, and the rehab I went through, and how that got me interested in nursing.

I still haven't made up my mind between nursing and teaching, though. Some of the guys I served with couldn't find Afghanistan on a map before they died there. There's so much ignorance. When I tell her I think I could make a difference as a history or geography teacher if nursing doesn't work out, she surprises me. I'm expecting her to make a pitch for the medical field, since this is where she's headed herself. Instead she says that the experiences I've had as a soldier would give me some real credibility with students in the classroom. That's sort of what I'm thinking, too. Students might actually pay attention to someone who has been through what I've been through when the topic of war comes up again, which it seems pretty likely to do with our Chickenhawk-in-Chief playing nuclear ping-pong with Kim Jong and doing his best to pick a fight with the insane Ayatollahs. Of course, he knows those bone spurs in his brain will keep him out of harm's way while guys like me go out to do the fighting and the dying.

Like a lot of people I meet, Alicia seems surprised that I wanted to serve, given the discrimination that we still face every day in this country. I tell her that I come from a long line of soldiers. My great-grandfather hit the beach at Anzio in World War II, my grandfather was in Vietnam, and my father was in the Gulf War. Before them I'm not so sure about, but my family has been in California for more than two hundred years, so I wouldn't be surprised if they fought in this country's wars before those, too. When people act like it's weird that Latinos want to serve in a country that is prejudiced against them, I like to remind them about one of my favorite movies. Next time you get a chance to watch *Saving Private Ryan*, check out the opening scene, when Ryan is an old man, kneeling in front of the rows and rows of crosses of his comrades who died in Normandy on D-Day. The name on the cross right in front of him is Mike Martinez. He's no relation to me, as far as I know, but as Ken Burns had to learn the hard way when he made his documentary, Latinos were a big part of *The Greatest Generation*. There were plenty of us who served in the war that saved the world.

Alicia asks if there is much discrimination in the service now. I tell her that of course there is some, there are always assholes in any group, but mostly the Army brings guys from different backgrounds together and gets us past our differences. I tell her about DeShaun, who bugged me at first with his East Coast sense of humor, but quickly became the best friend I've ever had. We pushed each other through Ranger camp and then served our first tour together. When we got leave, he invited me home to spend Thanksgiving in Newark with his family, who turned out to be just about the nicest people I've ever met.

"I was planning to return the favor and bring him out here to meet my family the next time we got leave."

"What happened?"

"He didn't make it that far. Didn't even make it to his second tour. He got killed stateside in a training accident when the helicopter he was in malfunctioned and went down."

"I'm so sorry," she says softly.

"That stuff happens more often than most people realize. In the Army you're at risk all the time—not just when you're in a firefight. Anyway, meeting him—and his family—was one of the best things that ever happened to me. I'll even admit I was probably a little bit of a racist before I met them. They were a big part of turning that around. Both of his parents have college degrees, and their encouragement is one of the reasons I'm going to college myself now, the first in my family to get this far. I tell them I'm doing it for DeShaun, too, since he won't get the chance."

When I flip the script and ask her about the discrimination she has faced here, she tells a familiar story.

"Is not so bad for me. I haven't had too much trouble. But whenever I go to a clothing store, especially if I go with Tori, my roommate who is black, the salespeople, if they are white or Asian, or sometimes even if they are Latino or black themselves—or the security people, if they have them—follow us around like we're going to steal something. Sometimes they even poke their heads into the changing room, like I'm going to put on a pair of panties or a bra and walk out with them on under my clothes. They assume I can't pay because of the color of my skin. Is humiliating. I don't even like to go shopping anymore."

"I'm sorry," I tell her. "You're right: no one should have

to go through that. But if you think we have a problem with discrimination here, go to Afghanistan some time. When you see the way women are abused over there or how shitty life is for the kids, it really makes you appreciate what we have here, in spite of stuff like that in stores. Here, we've turned eating into a spectator sport: we have contests where fat guys compete on ESPN to see who can eat the most hot dogs before they puke. We spend more money on dog food than we do to feed the world's children. Meanwhile, in Kabul, eight-year-olds are selling their sisters' pictures on the streets to try to scrape up enough protein to make it to nine."

She is still listening. "Do you think our soldiers are making things any better for them?"

"The whole idea of spreading our form of democracy around the world, I admit, that's kind of sketchy. I didn't meet too many people there who were interested in that. They were just trying to stay out of the Taliban's way and stay alive. People here, even the ones who grew up in the poorest neighborhoods or came here with nothing, have a million more chances to get somewhere in life than those people do. It's no wonder half the people in the world are trying to get here."

She nods. "People like me, you mean."

She talks a bit more about herself, and I hear the American Dream in every syllable. Came across the border with only the clothes on her back, and now she's planning to be a doctor. In how many countries in the world is that even possible? I don't know if she'll make it, considering all the obstacles she'll have to overcome, but it's clear that she's planning to take her best shot. She's kind of quiet, but she seems really determined and confident that she can do it.

When I ask more about her, she spends more time talking about that baby she found than about herself. I don't really know what to say when she talks again about wanting to take care of the baby. I can sort of relate. We saw homeless kids all the time in Afghanistan, and a couple of them used to follow me around sometimes, hoping for a chocolate bar or a soda. I gave them whatever I had. One guy in our outfit brought out his spare boots and just handed them over to a big kid who was barefoot. I saw a lot of stuff like that. You see on the news about all the atrocities, all the crimes that American soldiers committed over there—and that stuff happens, too—but I saw a thousand acts of kindness or compassion that nobody in the media was interested in reporting.

She asks if I ever thought about bringing one of those kids home with me. I tell her since I'm single, I didn't think about trying to do that. I've still got to get my education and put myself in a position to take care of myself before I take on kids, my own or anyone else's. I ask if the same isn't true for her as well.

"Isn't it hard enough going to school full-time and working full-time?"

"Is hard, but I manage."

"Seems like adding a baby would make it a thousand times harder."

"I have a support system where I live. We could share the responsibilities. The other girls are willing to help."

"Have any of you taken care of a baby before?"

"A little bit. I . . . had a baby niece. I helped take care of her for a little while, but . . . she died when we crossed the border."

For a minute I think she is going to cry. "Shit. I'm sorry."

She blinks away the tears. "When I see the stories on TV now about all the families being separated at the border and the little kids who are dying, it just brings back all these terrible memories. How can people be so cruel? How can they be so blind?"

"Is that what happened to your family?"

"Sort of. We had to leave in a hurry when my father thought he got this great opportunity to bring us here—me, my mom, and my niece, I mean. My older sisters were already married, so they stayed in Mexico. One of them, Rosa, had a baby, Carmelita, who was sick all the time. The guy she married is a Jehovah's Witness, and he would not let her be vaccinated. My mother persuaded Rosa to let us try to bring Carmelita here with us, to get help for her, but—"

She chokes up again and stops.

"I know a little bit about Jehovah's Witnesses. I'm surprised your brother-in-law would let her go."

"He didn't know. Rosa didn't tell him. We basically kidnaped Carmelita. Rosa knew it was her baby's only chance, but she got sicker, right after we crossed, and we could not get help for her in time. She died before we—I mean, they—could get her to a hospital. When they tried, my parents were arrested and sent back to Mexico. I didn't go with them to try to get help, or I would have been deported, too. They had persuaded a cousin to take care of me here until I could find a job and take care of myself."

I nod but can think of nothing to say. She looks like she's going to cry again.

"All I could think about when I saw that baby on the floor in the café was what happened to my niece. A baby is just so helpless. We have to help them if we can. Now we have these crazy people trying to say that vaccination kills babies—my roommate has heard this in her church. Is just the opposite."

I nod again. This I can respond to. "There was a speaker in the quad on campus last month putting out that nonsense. Now we even have measles again, after nearly eliminating it. That kind of ignorance is the way kids get killed."

She checks the time on her phone—the first time she's pulled it out since we sat down—and says she has to get to class. I know it's a shit transition from measles, but I ask her if she wants to go with me to see a movie.

I figure she'll probably say between work and school, let alone trying to find this baby, she doesn't have time, but she surprises me again: "What movie do you want to see?"

This one I'm ready for.

"Whatever you want to see."

Okay, I'm hoping for not a cartoon superhero, not some godawful chick flick like *Dear John*, the all-time favorite of the last girl I went out with, and not some sappy romcom where you know for sure from the opening credits that the main actor and main actress will fall in love even if they hate each other's guts in the first scene. That doesn't leave much else to choose from these days. Sometimes I wonder who's more pathetic, the morons who make most of today's movies or the morons who watch them. At least the morons who make them are getting paid. On the other hand, even if somebody spends two years and a hundred million dollars to make a piece of crap, it only takes two hours to watch it.

The funny thing is I've always loved movies. I'm taking a film class right now, along with history, to sort of balance out the math and science I have to grind through if I go for nursing. I'm starting to notice a lot of stuff the teacher talks about—camera angles and cuts and soundtrack cues—that I never paid too much attention to before. Of course, some of the time what I notice is how boring the movie she's showing is. That *Open City*? Jesus, put me in an open grave before you ask me to watch that again. Fortunately, not all of her picks are that bad. She's trying to show us that a movie can be more than just mindless entertainment.

"I don't like to watch explosions and a lot of violence," Alicia says now.

"I've seen enough of those myself."

"There are lots of good films from Mexico, but they don't always play in the theaters here."

It's time for an embarrassing admission. "I don't speak Spanish. But I can always read the subtitles."

"I'm not insisting. Is just an idea."

"We'll figure something out."

She smiles, and I officially fall in love. We set a date, and she agrees to let me pick her up. She leaves me with a gentle piece of advice: "You really should learn to speak Spanish. Either nursing or teaching, is a big help."

Maybe you can teach me some of what you know I manage to keep to myself as I watch her head off to class before I head for mine.

It's the best I've felt since I kissed Afghanistan goodbye.

CHAPTER 12

MARTHA

Grandpa Jack is the only one who isn't thrilled about the idea of bringing a new baby to our house. It's hard to believe anybody wouldn't want to welcome a new baby, that's God's greatest gift to us, but you have to understand what he has been through.

Grandma Vi says he was never the same after he came back from the war. Even though they got divorced a long time ago, she let him come back last year and live in her garage, he had no place else to stay after his mobile home burned up in that big fire they had up north. She says he's not a bad person, he just drinks too much. I pray for him all the time. You can't really blame him for drinking to try to forget about all the terrible stuff that happened to he and his friends in the war.

His first night in Vietnam—he didn't tell Grandma Vi about this until years later, when she tried to get him to stop drinking— enemy soldiers snuck into the tent he was sleeping in, then slit the throats of the three other guys he was sharing with. They didn't even wake him up, they left him alive to see this when he woke up and then tell everybody else about it. Can you even imagine going through something like that? How do you go to sleep the next night after *that* happens?

According to Grandma Vi, Grandpa Jack said many times he wished it was him that got his throat cut and got it over with on his first day, instead of what he went through for the next three years. What I never figured out is why he reenlisted after he finished his first time, that just doesn't make any sense to me. Why would you go back to war when you could come home and live a normal life and try to forget about it?

Instead he kind of brought the war home with him, I'll give you an example of what I mean. One time when I was about nine, I was sitting on the porch with him—this was before Grandma Vi divorced him and kicked him out of the house, and before the first time I ran away—and we saw a neighbor stopping on our lawn with a big dog. I love dogs, I've never been afraid of them, so I started to run out to pet it. Grandpa Jack told me to stay where I was, then he went inside and came back out with his shotgun. Meanwhile, the dog did its business on our lawn and was pawing to cover it up. The neighbor said something about he forgot his pooper-scooper.

Grandpa Jack says to him, "Well, in that case, you'll just have to pick it up with your hands, won't you?"

The neighbor is completely shocked, he says, "You're shitting me, right? You can't be serious."

Grandpa Jacks points his shotgun right at the neighbor. "Do I look like I'm not serious? Pick it up."

The neighbor searches his pockets, for a piece of tissue I guess, but he doesn't find anything.

"I don't have any paper with me. Can you at least give me something?"

"Maybe you should've thought of that before you left the house with that fucking mutt. Pick it up."

I'm sitting there with my eyes practically popping out of my head, I start to say I'll go into the house to get something, but without even looking over at me Grandpa Jack tells me to sit still. He gestures with the shotgun toward the poop. And the neighbor actually stoops over and picks it up in his bare hands, then starts looking around for something to dump it in.

"Where's your garbage can?"

"That's not my garbage."

"Well, what the hell am I supposed to do with it now?"

You'll never believe what Grandpa Jack says next.

"Guess you'll just have to eat it."

"Are you out of your—"

"Go on. Take a bite," Grandpa Jack says. "It won't kill you. On the other hand, this shotgun might."

The neighbor looks at him like he's completely crazy, which in a way I suppose he is, but Grandpa Jack just stares at him and points the shotgun again. And you know what? The neighbor actually does it, takes a bite, then right away he drops the poop and starts to puke. It was just disgusting! Then he starts to run away, and the dog starts to run, too, and the neighbor trips over the leash and falls and lands right in the middle of the mess. When he gets up and tries to scramble away, he trips over the dog again and falls splat on the sidewalk, Grandpa Jack starts cackling like he's watching one of those crazy old movies with the Three Stooges or Abbott and Costello that I used to watch on TV with him all the time.

Now Grandpa Jack's got poop *and* puke on his lawn, but he looks like he couldn't be happier with the way things turned out. He winks at me.

"What do you think, sweetheart? Maybe next time he'll remember his pooper-scooper."

When I tell Grandma Vi about it later, she just shakes her head and says Grandpa Jack has done lots crazier things than that, she says our neighbor is lucky him and his dog didn't get a face full of buckshot.

We've got dogs pooping all over our neighborhood now— but I never did see *that* dog poop on our lawn again.

CHAPTER 13

NATALIE

Usually, you assume families will try hard to put their best foot forward when you show up for an on-site visit. This isn't a surprise inspection or anything of that nature. I *hate* pop-ins. You never know what kind of chaos you're going to walk into or get caught up in: on separate occasions I've had a knife, a gun, a bottle, and a tomahawk brandished at me, and so many lawsuits threatened that I lost count a long time ago. But of course it's the best way to find out what the environment's really like—there's no time to hide the gin bottles or the crack pipe when the social worker shows up out of the blue.

This isn't one of those, though. I had called ahead and confirmed a specific time. I arrive a few minutes early, as per my normal operating procedure.

The first thing I see is the garage door open and a senior citizen sitting in a rocking chair in his longjohns and a veteran's cap, smoking a cigarette and cleaning a shotgun with a rag that looks like a remnant of an American flag. A bottle of whiskey sits within his reach. He is staring at me with open hostility.

"You the one from the government?"

"I'm with CPS, yes. I'm here to—"

"I know what the hell you're here to do."

"Are you part of the family proposing to adopt?"

"Part of the family? I guess so. I guess you could say I'm the crazy part that got banished to the garage. Baby won't be bunking with me, you let the crazies in the house keep it."

I frown at this. "Crazies? My records show the girls are all college students who are doing reasonably well in their—"

"They all got some book learning, but that don't mean they got a lick of common sense. I bet you got a college degree yourself."

"I have a master's degree, yes."

"Think that means you're smart?"

"It means . . . I did well enough in school to—"

"Raised any babies of your own? How many kids you got?"

"Well, none actually, but—"

He's giving me an incredulous look, which I've seen from many others before: *a black woman with no kids? She must be a lesbian.*

"—that's hardly the point of this—"

"Where the hell do you get off telling other people how to raise babies if you ain't done it yourself? You think you learn how to be a parent by reading a goddam book?"

I'm not even at the doorstep yet, and already I'm under assault. I try to adjust on the fly. "Are you a parent yourself, Mr.— "

"Damn right, I'm a parent. I'm a grandparent, too. And you know what? I know fuck-all about raising a kid. Had two of my own, least that's who my ex-wife in there in her wheelchair blamed for 'em. My boy, supposed to be my pride and joy, was a world-class fuck-up who got kicked out of every school he went to and fired from every job he ever had, then threw away his life. You invest your own life, you sacrifice everything you want for yourself to raise him, you potty-train him, you watch him pop his pimples in the mirror, you teach him how to drive your car—which the selfish son-of-a-bitch brings back with an empty gas tank *every* damn time, until one night he gets wasted and crashes it into a fucking telephone pole. So you take him to the hospital and the docs patch him up and you help him through a thousand hours of rehab until he can almost walk again without assistance—and then the fucker goes and kills himself! This is my reward for giving up my own fucking life to raise him."

I don't know what to say. I've dealt with lots of family suicides over the years, of course, but this is thrust at me so abruptly that I'm at a loss. He isn't finished.

"My girl, on the other hand, my precious princess, is still alive somewhere, as far as I know, and no doubt still putting out for any man with a few bucks to buy her a fix. Putting out for any woman, too, most likely. She was a meth whore who hit the streets and started dropping babies when she was sixteen. One of them lives here now, little Miss Martha. Been down that trail herself before she found Jesus in some parking lot and came home with her tail between her legs to sponge off my ex."

My head is spinning as I try to process all of this before I ring the doorbell. "Your ex? Is she the one who owns this house?"

He laughs. "The bank owns this house and her ass. Few years ago she let one of them smooth-talking pretty boys on TV sell her on taking out a reverse mortgage. Biggest scam going, and Vi fell for it, just like she fell for vinyl siding and earthquake insurance. Let me ask you this: California cracks in half and drops into the Pacific Ocean, you think there's gonna be any cash left in the economy to pay off any insurance policies?"

It's a question I hadn't considered, nor expected to. Clearly it's time to move on to the next phase of the inspection. "I think I'll just head inside now and—"

"Maybe you should adopt this baby yourself. Get some actual on-the-job training, you might learn how to help other folks cope a little better when their faggot son borrows a dress from his drug addict whore sister and steals his father's pistol, which he never bothered to learn how to hit anything with before and you figured he didn't even know how to load, and then, right here in this house, blows his brains out on the first try. And doesn't even leave a goddam note to tell you why."

Now my head is *really* spinning. I think a full rotation like in *The Exorcist* may not be out of the question. I'm at a loss for what to say.

"Thank you for the career counseling," I manage. Irony has never been my strong suit.

"It's free. I don't charge nothin' for my advice. How much they pay you for yours?"

The salaries of all state employees are a matter of public record. You can go on transparency.com and look up any of us. Just be prepared for a shock to your system when you see what your tax dollars are providing in annual income for correctional officers with their high school educations and their double-overtime triple-shifts; for pension fund managers with guaranteed salaries of several hundred thousand even when their investments lose money for the rest of us; or for the doctors at the county hospital, some of whom failed in private practice, now pulling in more than a million. I've taken a look myself, obviously, and, even though of course I never went into this profession to get rich, it's somewhat disheartening to compare my own compensation. I make forty dollars an hour, about eighty thousand a year, barely enough to qualify for a mortgage of my own if I needed one now.

I decide not to risk more derision by sharing this information. Instead I'm going to try to end this conversation on a positive note. It's a tactic I learned a long time ago, one that doesn't always work, but always worth a try. It's something I picked up, not in any classroom, conference, or workshop, not from any professor, colleague, or supervisor, but from my father, who spent his career as a postman. He is in my mind even now, as he is so often since his passing, his simple, common sense lessons still informing my work and my life.

I point at the cap that my interrogator is wearing.

"I see you are a Vietnam veteran."

"Damn right, I am. Three tours. I didn't rape any babies or set fire to any orphanages, if that was going to be your next question."

"It wasn't my next question. I was just going to thank you for your service and tell you that my dad served there, too."

"That right? What unit? He see any combat?"

"I don't think so. He was a clerk-typist. He didn't like to talk about it much."

"Shit, I don't blame him. I wouldn't talk about it much either if I spent the war as a damn office monkey when other guys was gettin' shot to shit or scramblin' to stay out of pungi pits."

One of the books my father encouraged me to read in order to understand his experience was Tim O'Brien's *Going after Cacciato*. I don't know if anyone reads it anymore, but one of the parts I remember most clearly was about the ratio of support to combat personnel during the Vietnam War. My father was in the vast majority who never fired a weapon at the enemy. It wasn't exactly something to be ashamed of.

"He get drafted, or did he volunteer to win the war in the typing pool?"

"His lottery number was eleven. He enlisted when he knew he was going to be drafted. He had learned how to type to get ready for college, which he never got a chance to go to, but maybe having that skill spared him the dangers that you and others faced. Maybe it even saved his life."

He shrugs.

I continue: "In a weird way, even though he hated war, I think he was proud that he did his part . . . however small. The media talk so much about the one percent who own just about everything in our country, but the other one percent who serve in the military, people like the two of you, deserve to be recognized a lot more. Who knows, maybe you even crossed paths with him when you were over there."

"I didn't hold hands with too many typists when we was out huntin' gooks in the Mekong Delta."

People are always telling me I should use my smile more:

it's my best feature, they say. I suppose that's sort of a back-handed compliment, a way of letting me know that my other features aren't as prepossessing. I try a smile now.

"Well, maybe he processed your paycheck or something."

"Some great paycheck. You got any idea how much they paid us for what we did over there?"

"I know it couldn't possibly be enough. I just wanted to let you know that I appreciate your sacrifice."

He nods. "At least your old man didn't take a powder to Canada like plenty of other shitheels did. You gonna put me in your report?"

I smile again. "I don't see how I could leave you out."

He nods and goes back to his cigarette, his shotgun, and his bottle. I let out a deep breath and go to the door to see who or what awaits me inside.

CHAPTER 14

MOUA

So I'm sure you were wondering how a good little Hmong girl like me, with straight A's since like the second grade, got involved in my current occupation. It was actually a classmate at my high school who got me started, or gave me the idea anyway. You might have heard about her. She was in the local news, even made the San Francisco newspaper, and might even have been a national story for all I know.

What happened was the student newspaper at our school ran this front-page article about her because she was living on her own and supporting herself—by working in the porn industry. She got her start doing some lingerie modeling. One thing led to another, and she got offered a lot of money to take her clothes off in some movies. Of course, a lot of the other students at the high school have watched these on their phones or computers, especially after the article made her famous. I'll bet plenty of the teachers there have taken a look, too. The school district had a total shitfit over it and tried to stop the article from being printed in the first place, but the faculty advisor for the paper is this real kick-ass maverick who isn't intimidated by anything. She's had tenure like forever, and she doesn't let anyone tell her how to do her job. They've tried to fire her a dozen times in the past for articles that she refused to censor, although maybe nothing quite as embarrassing to the school as this one. She just tells them to read the First Amendment and "Take me to court." They wind up backing down every time.

At the time the big story came out, I was getting even more crap than usual from my mom at home, and I knew I had to get out of there before *I* made the news for suicide or homicide. The article got me thinking: nobody's going to pay money to see my body in an ad or a movie, but maybe there was a way to use my imagination instead and still cash in.

So a confession: I've never actually like *done* the dirty deed. Everything you need to know is online really, and it's a lot less messy as far as I can tell. I may be the only eighteen year-old virgin left in the Western Hemisphere (unless you count Martha, who got herself revirginized by Pastor Greg), but the real deal looks pretty disgusting to me. On the phone, on the other hand, there's no exchange of bodily fluids, no risk of STDs, no possibility of getting pregnant, and no worries about jealous wives or girlfriends tracking you down and beating you up or suing you for alienating the affections of the jerk-offs they can't satisfy. It's the ultimate form of *safe sex*, and it sounded perfect for me. I found a quick way to pay for my own 900 number, and I made back my investment in like two weeks. It's all been gravy since. Keep that in mind if anyone ever tries to tell you than porn doesn't pay.

Another great thing about the phone sex biz is that you don't have to worry about shelling out for a boob job and getting butchered by some plastic surgeon who finished last in his class at the Tegucigalpa Quack Factory. If some pinhead with a penis probably the size of a peanut needs to believe he's putting it to a babe with forty-four inches on top, all I have to do is say the magic words, and *voila*, I'm racked like Stormy Daniels as far as he can tell. Truly, where's the harm? I'm still waiting for an explanation from one of those concerned citizen role model-types who get their panties in a twist over any type of pornography but want the corporations they invest in to continue to be able to peddle their tobacco products and their weapons all over the planet. As far as I know, an AT&T-enhanced DIY handjob never gave anyone cancer or blew his head off. If some of those guys who run down to the pawn shop to pick up their artillery and then shoot up elementary schools just gave me a call and got off on that instead, we'd all be a lot safer, and a lot of little snotnoses would still be running around driving their parents crazy instead of dead before they even got their driver's license and the chance to *really* drive them crazy.

So anyway I'm hooked up with this extra-kinky client, who seems like a good candidate for tomorrow's headlines if I don't chill him out, when I hear the doorbell ring. I remember, *crap, I forgot to tell Alicia about the social worker who called yesterday to schedule an appointment.* I'd gotten a business call on my cell right after I'd picked up the landline when she called, and I just got too busy making some money to write a note or let Alicia know. I tell my pretend pedophile to play with himself for a minute now, and I run to the door to let our guest/inspector in.

I heard in my Sociology class that social workers tend to burn out and quit after about ten years on the job. Taking babies away from parents who abuse them, and deciding who else will give them a better life with all the psychos out there trying to make some easy money, that's got to be a tough gig. This one, though, looks like she passed the ten-year mark a long time ago. She's about forty-five, black, plain Jane type, not much make-up, didn't spend much time on her hair or clothes, too busy saving the world, I guess.

She gives me a smile when I pull the door open. She's not so plain, almost pretty, when she smiles. She has nice teeth, like everyone else in the world except me and my siblings. Mom wouldn't spring for braces for any of us. At least mine didn't come in sideways like a couple of my brothers' did. Out of the corner of my eye I see that the g-pa has the garage door open, and he's sitting out there in his underwear, sipping whiskey and playing Army again. I figure she must have met him on the way in, and I can't help wondering what a fabulous first impression *that* must have made. She's got to be wondering if we're all as batshit as he is.

"You must be Moua," she says, either remembering from our minute-long phone conversation or showing that she's done her homework, before I can introduce myself. "I'm Natalie Robinson from CPS."

I let her in, sit her down in the family room, and run to find Alicia, who is getting some grooming tips from Tori in the bathroom before her big date with Mr. Right, the first guy Alicia's said "yes" to going out with in all the time I've known her. I have to get back to my customer, so I keep it short, eat some shit with my apology, and point them to the inspector. Tori gives me a dirty look like I just sat on her fiancé's face; Alicia just nods and goes right out to meet the woman who will decide if she gets a chance to raise her baby. Meanwhile, Martha gets wind of what's happening, pushes the g-ma into the room in her chair, and asks if everyone would like to join her in a quick prayer before the shooting starts. Then the doorbell rings again, and I'm guessing Alicia's guy has arrived to pick her up. I don't go to answer it, though; I've got to pick up my call and pretend to be ten again before I lose a chunk of next month's rent. I almost wish I could stay to watch the show. Welcome to the nuthouse!

CHAPTER 15

EDUARDO

Expect The Unexpected (Part 2).

I'll tell you the truth: I wasn't too thrilled about the movie Alicia had picked out for our first real date, a matinee no less. Like I said, though, I was okay with taking it slow, and I was ready to sit through two hours of whatever in order to get off to a good start with her. It turns out that meeting the cast of characters she lives with is probably a hell of lot more entertaining than anything we would have seen on the silver screen.

I feel sort of sorry for Ms. Robinson. She seems okay, sincere and all, but man, what a way to meet a family looking to adopt a baby. Somebody should have handed her a scorecard before she sat down. That chick Tori, what a handful! Beautiful, almost as gorgeous as Alicia, but the mouth on her! It's like she's interrogating the social worker instead of the other way around. Alicia keeps trying to smooth things over and calm her down, get back to answering Ms. Robinson's questions. Then the old lady in the wheelchair, the grandmother, starts in with all the Bible stuff and Pharaoh's daughter finding Moses in the reed basket and none of us would be here today if she had just shoved him back into the river. Bithia. I haven't heard that name for a *long* time.

Ms. Robinson keeps her cool through the whole deal. She explains that there will be some serious complications with the adoption request, as I had figured, because Alicia is illegal. With Trump's Gestapo trying hard to round her up and send her back to Mexico, it's not exactly the ideal situation for placing a baby. Martha explains that her grandmother will be the official adoptive parent, with all of the girls in the house helping out with taking care of the baby. Ms. Robinson looks at me for a second, and I wonder if she's trying to figure out how or where I fit into all of this. I'm sort of wondering the same thing myself. Am I ready to get involved with a girl who spends half of her life working, the other half going to school, and now wants to add a baby to her schedule? How much help is she going to get from an old woman in a wheelchair, even if she has a direct line to Jesus? How much help is this Tori going to be? It's one o'clock in the afternoon, and she looks like she's ready to hit every night club in town.

A short, skinny Asian chick steps out of a room down the hall, closes the door behind her, and joins the conversation. This is Moua, I learn. She seems to be really up on all the laws about adoption. She makes the point that living with this family would be a much better option than the circumstances the baby they want was born into. She also raises the question of what happens if the birth mother wants a do-over and shows up to claim the kid. No one else has thought of this, or at least nobody brought it up before. It's a good question. I wonder how often it happens to screw up the adoption process.

Ms. Robinson acknowledges that the birth mother could resurface at some point but also says that this conversation is getting ahead of itself. First, she has to make the determination about the suitability of the environment for the baby to be placed here. It seems she has some reservations about the old soldier she saw bivouacked in the garage. I saw him, too, but didn't stop to talk to him when I pulled up. He looks like he's lived through some serious shit, that's for sure.

"Maybe we should invite him in to join the conversation," Ms. Robinson suggests.

"Jack Mackey is not allowed inside this house," the grandmother says, and it's clear that she means it. "He stays in the garage, by the grace of God. He will have absolutely no contact with this baby, you may rest assured of that. The man has served his country with honor, so we abide his presence, but he has no business ever interacting with any children after what he did to his own—*our* own."

The grandmother puts her head down like she's going to cry. Martha looks like she's going to cry, too. Alicia looks like she just wants this interview to be over before someone spills the beans about what Jack did to his kids.

Ms. Robinson stands up. "I think I've heard enough for today. I'll be back in touch soon."

Moua speaks up again: "Did we pass?"

"It wasn't a test," Ms. Robinson says. "Just a preliminary investigation."

I can't decide if that's more like a yes or more like a no. Tori is shaking her head in contempt, as if to say how could anyone not instantly give the seal of approval to any family that she is part of? Alicia catches me looking at Tori, and I wonder if there's a flicker of jealousy in her eyes. Nothing to worry about there, I want to tell her, before I remind myself not to go too fast: your roommate is amazing, she looks like a damn movie star, but you are the one I am here for—with or without the baby that you might or might not get.

CHAPTER 16

ALICIA

I'm sorry about the movie I've made him miss, but I'm glad he stays. Even though I'm just barely getting to know him, it's really comforting to have him there in the room when Ms. Robinson is checking us out. I like that he is willing to sit and listen, and not jump in and try to take charge or tell all these *locas* what to do, like so many men would do. Papi always says a man should listen more than he speaks—and then speak with his actions, with his work, not so much with his words. Who knows what might have happened if Martha's grandpa had been allowed to come in and talk? Probably I'd be on my way back to Mexico in handcuffs by now and the baby would be assigned to somebody, *any*body, else.

Afterward, I am just hoping the whole situation hasn't completely turned Eduardo off. I am so happy when he calls me again the next day.

"Have you heard anything yet about your baby?"

"Not yet. We're a little worried about the effect Martha's grandpa might have had on the social worker."

"The way her grandmother spoke about him, I was beginning to wonder if there's a bloody chainsaw out in the garage somewhere."

"I don't think he ever abused his kids or anything. He just didn't know how to be a father."

"It's a big club. A lot of guys in the service talked about what shitheads their fathers were and how much they hated them. Made me appreciate mine more."

I ask him to tell me more about his father.

"After he bought into the nursery, he kept his maintenance job with the school district. He has basically worked two full-time jobs, eighty hours a week, ever since, to support our family."

"My papi is the same. He is always working. When he is finished with his own work, he goes and helps my sisters. He does for them all the chores that their husbands say they are too busy to do, when really they are just too lazy. He is always helping someone. I miss him so much."

"It must be really hard for you to be here without your family."

I don't allow myself to say how hard this is. "Of course. But I have my Martha family, too. I'm really lucky to have a place to live and a job."

"Aren't you worried that this adoption business will . . ."

"Expose me? Get me sent back, too?"

"It seems like a risk, anyway."

"Of course. But I just feel that I have to do something for this baby. I believe we are on this Earth for one reason: to help others. We can't live just for ourselves."

He asks me if I got my philosophy in church. I have been waiting for him to ask me about this, like most guys I meet would have by now. Even though there is a Jehovah's Witness in my own family, and Eduardo knows something about this religion, I am guessing that he has been raised Catholic, like me and most other Mexicans. I wonder if he will ask me to go to church with him, like Martha and her grandmother are always doing. I wonder also how he will feel about me when I give him the answer. I am not sure over the telephone is the best place to have this conversation, but I decide to just get it over with and tell him the truth.

"Not so much," I say. "Mami and Papi still go to church every week, and they always want to know if I am going, too, so I tell a big truth and a little lie to make them happy: I say that school and work keep me busy, but I go when I can."

"It's not hard to guess which part is the lie."

I wonder if he is judging me now. "The truth is I never got back into the habit of going to church once I was here and separated from them. When Carmelita died, I just couldn't understand how the God my parents believe in could let that happen to a little baby. She didn't live long enough to learn anything about Jesus or getting saved or anything like that. Does that mean she doesn't get to go to Heaven? It just didn't make sense to me. I hope I'm not making you mad when I say that."

"I'm not mad, just interested," he tells me. "Actually, I feel the same way. After some of the stuff I saw in Afghanistan, I've never had much faith in a God that would let that go on. You see a little kid with his head blown off by a mortar round, you don't exactly want to fall on your knees and praise Jesus for calling in the strike. And of course you see the complete insanity of the radical Islamists everywhere you go over there, the crazy rules they make up and enforce, the way they treat women and kids. They don't even want girls to go to school. It kind of makes you wonder about the mental health of the religious extremists on our side of the world—the ones trying to get rid of vaccination, like you mentioned, and trying to beat back evolution and sex education and all the other kinds of progress that science has created to bring us out of the Dark Ages. So no, I'm not mad that you don't go to church. We don't have to have faith in God in order to want to help other people."

"Thank you." I suppose it might seem very strange to some people, but I'm so relieved to hear all this, that he doesn't believe in God either. "Is good to know you don't think I'm a bad person."

"You're the best person I've met in a long time. Most people just care about themselves. I really admire you for what you're trying to do to help that baby."

His words give me a very warm feeling, but I decide that's enough serious talk for now. Time to play. "My friend Tori admires *you*. Did you notice her checking you out?"

"Not really."

"You don't have to lie. I know she's really hot. She always says she only dates black guys, but she said she might make an exception for you."

"Thanks for letting me know, but she's not the one I'm interested in."

I'll confess I kind of tingle when he says this. He seems to know just the right thing to say. Mami always warned me that men will say anything to get what they want from you, but he seems to be different from the other guys I've met. Maybe his time serving in the Army made him more mature. I can't even imagine the horrible things he saw there. Although the Army didn't seem to do anything to grow up Martha's grandpa. I guess he saw some pretty horrible things, too. I know that many women are serving in the military now, some even in combat, but I could never make that choice. I'm glad I will never have to find out what fighting in a war would do to me.

Eduardo asks if I want to try again to see a movie. I *really* need to study this weekend, but I'm almost ready to agree to an evening date. I can hardly wait to hear what Tori will say about that. Maybe she will volunteer to be our chaperone!

CHAPTER 17

TORI

Army background, that don't impress me none. Learn a lot of violent shit in there, go off to war in some fuckhole in the desert or the jungle and bring it home with you. I got a cousin still so fucked up from serving in Iraq, he talkin' to the rocks and the trees. Made it home in one piece, unlike some of his friends, but never did hold a steady job or get off the drugs he got started on over there. You fixin' to find a dependable man, Army background 'bout the last place you need to be looking. I don't tell her this shit, though. Best let her find out for herself. Tell a girl a guy ain't right for her, best way to push her right into his bed.

He is cute, I'll give him that. I had to mess with Alicia a little bit about takin' him off her hands. Funny hearin' her talk about the muscles on him, like it's the first time she ever noticed. I never thought she even cared about that shit. I'll bet she got some happy fingers tonight, when she start thinkin' 'bout those guns on him. I like to look at them, too, like to feel 'em squeeze me tight, but I told her muscles don't earn you shit on payday. Guys be in the gym working out all the time and forget to go to their day job, bring home some damn money. Muscles don't put no dinner on the table, 'less you make it with the pros.

Now she sayin' he maybe wants to be a teacher. That ain't even hardly a step up from Army. Shit, teachers be goin' out on strike every other minute just to get paid enough to make their rent. Can't even afford to buy a house in the town they teachin' in. Don't make sense for Alicia to shoot for that shit. With her face, her figure, all that perfect hair, she got to score her a surgeon, or at least some kind of doctor.

Now a girl who look like Martha, on the other hand, might make sense to settle for a teacher. Maybe even set her sights. Better off doin' that than wastin' her time on the phonies she meet at that damn church, always talkin' to her about stayin' after services to work on *special projects* and such. Give me a fuckin' break. Poor girl think it was Jesus who saved her. Ask me, it was Grammy who gets the credit for that, takin' her in off the street, givin' her another chance. Too bad Grammy had to use all that Bible shit to back it up. Martha be still all worried about the shit she done in the past, wantin' to tell you every last detail, wantin' to be forgiven for every little thing. I tell her we've all done shit we're not proud of. It don't mean you got to confess to everyone you meet. Hell, the ones you confessin' to has done their share of evil shit, too.

I tell Alicia to leave the teacher nerds for Martha to pick from. "You be livin' in some pitiful apartment or duplex right next to a laundromat, you marry a loser with a job like that."

"I didn't say I was going to marry him. I said I might go out with him again."

"Wastin' your time, girl."

"So how did it go for *you* last night?"

Okay, I guess she finally gonna shut up about Eduardo. My turn. We ain't talked since Jerome brought me home. She know I come home early, though.

"I heard from Moua it was no Pinto he picked you up in."

"Oh, nothin' like that: 2019 Escalade. Fine-ass automobile."

"Sounds like a good start."

"Could've been worse. Only problem is, I find out pretty quick it ain't his."

"Oh?"

"Belong to his mama."

"Oh. Well, maybe he borrowed it to impress you. Or maybe his own car was in the shop?"

"Guess again."

"Oh."

"He don't own a car of his own."

"Well, that's not the end of the world, is it? Lots of people can't afford a car yet. You're looking at one of them, remember? Maybe he's saving up to buy one, like I am."

Alicia don't hardly even buy clothes for herself, let alone a car. She sendin' more money home to Mexico to help out her folks than she savin' or spendin' on herself. Jerome ain't got that excuse.

"He not just drivin' his mama's car, he livin' in her damn house. Twenty-eight years old, and he don't even have a roof of his own. After we had dinner, which he didn't exactly dazzle me with, takin' me to Rubio's, he ask if we can come back here to watch TV or somethin' in my room. Of course, I know what he really want to do in there. I told him he got a better shot with a sidewalk 'ho in the backseat of his mama's Cadillac."

"That must have made him happy."

"What I want to know is, where did we get all these man-boys that don't want to grow up? They happy to lay back and let their mamas take care of 'em, pay the rent, pay the Comcast and the PG&E, buy the groceries, wash their clothes. Shit, I'll bet Jerome's mama even make his bed for him."

"I guess you won't be finding out for yourself any time soon."

"Hell, no. I told him to get a job, get a car, get a crib, then give me a call. And don't take me to no damn Rubio's if by some miraculous act of generosity or stupidity I decide to give you another chance, which don't count on anyway."

"Sounds like you got your point across."

"Oh, yeah. I won't hear from that dude no more. When you might be goin' out with Eduardo again?"

She shrugs but doesn't seem worried about it. I guess they haven't made a plan yet. At least this guy got her mind off that baby she found for a minute. When I ask her again what she gonna do about that, she say Moua got a nibble on that fake reward shit she posted on Facebook. Askin' for trouble there, you ask me, with that sneaky-ass Asian shit.

I'll bet that tightass social work sister would be real interested in findin' out how our little local mastermind cover her room and board.

CHAPTER 18

ALICIA

I recognize her right away when she comes into the café.

The *gringa* has cut her hair short, like a man's, and she has tried to dye it. She isn't looking quite as ghetto as the first time I saw her, but I know it is her. She knows I know it, too.

She can't look me in the eye when she speaks. She looks at her filthy shoes instead.

"The message said there's a reward. Do you have the money with you?"

"I can get the money."

"It'll have to be cash. I don't have a checking account."

"I can get you cash. But you have to help me find the baby. Come sit down over here with my friends and we'll figure it out."

She looks over at the table where Moua and Eduardo are waiting for us. Maybe she is trying to figure out if Eduardo is an undercover cop waiting to arrest her.

"I rather talk just to you. Can you give me some of the money now? I haven't had anything to eat in two days."

"Come and sit down and we'll get you something to eat. We'll get you your money, too, eventually. No one is here to judge you or punish you. We just want to help your baby. What's your name, anyway?"

"I'm Morgan."

She follows me to the table with her head down. I introduce everyone to her. Eduardo stands up—he's such a gentleman—

and Moua sort of cracks up over it, like he's greeting the Queen at Buckingham Palace instead of a girl off the street. I tell him Morgan needs food, and he goes to order it from Clara. She's way ahead of us and has a plate full of tacos ready to hand off to him. Our guest inhales a couple of them without taking time to wash her hands first, and I remember what it's like to be really, really hungry, something I haven't felt for quite a while. My heart goes out to her, in spite of what she did. I wonder how many other girls have done the same.

She drains a big coke in a couple of swallows and reaches for another taco. Clara comes over, hands on her hips, to join our conversation. Morgan almost looks at her.

"These are really good. Thank you."

"I'm glad you like 'em, honey. You was in too much of a rush to taste our food last time."

"I know you all must hate me for what I did," Morgan says.

"Could've just dropped her at the hospital, you know," Clara tells her. "The laws says you don't even have to leave your name."

Morgan's head goes right back down. "I didn't know that. I figured somebody here would know what to do with my baby. Anyone could take better care of her than I could."

My heart melts again. As much as I hate what she did, I don't hate her. I just want to help.

"Do you know what happened to her?" she asks. "My boyfriend followed me here before—when I . . . left her—and tried to get her back, but he got arrested that night."

I look at Eduardo. He shoots me a little smile. Now we have the missing piece of our *cómo nos conocemos* story.

Clara goes back to the kitchen. Moua speaks up, tells all we know, keeps it short: the cops, the hospital, the adoption agency, CPS. "Then CPS sent Ms. Robinson to check us out when we reached out to help the baby."

"Us? We? What do you mean?"

"We share a house with a couple of other students," Moua explains. "Alicia wants us to adopt your baby."

Morgan looks at Eduardo. He smiles at her. "I'm not one of the roommates. Just along for moral support. Looks like you could use a refill."

He picks up the coke glass and goes to refill it, giving us girls some space. I tell myself to watch out or I could fall in love with this man.

It's time to *confesar algo* about the cash, which I don't have, not even close. I tell her we can make the payments in weekly installments over a couple of months if she agrees to sign over the baby to our care. It feels really weird to propose a transaction like this, almost like human trafficking, buying a baby, but Moua explains that she has researched it and thinks we can probably get custody if the birth mother and the adoption agency agree. The agency, obviously, won't need to know about the cash.

"That's just between us chickens," she says.

I wince a little at that. Moua's got an off-the-chain sense of humor and picks the strangest times to try it out.

Our guest doesn't seem offended. She eats another taco and reaches for the glass that Eduardo set back on the table before stepping aside again.

"Are you sure I won't get in trouble?"

Now comes the tricky part. "We're not in a position to make any promises about that," I admit.

"I've been to jail a couple of times. I don't ever want to go back. I *really* don't want to go to prison."

I see Clara, standing near the cash register now, still listening, and shaking her head. I can almost hear her thinking: *Maybe you should've thought of that before you spread your legs and ditched your baby.*

Eduardo comes back over to the table, looks at me as if for permission to join us again. I nod, and he surprises me by taking my hand, the first time he has touched me. He nods at me then, as if to encourage me to go ahead with what we discussed if the real mother turned up.

I give it *mi mejor tiro*: "If we can help your baby, that's the main thing. All of us will testify to help you"—I look over to see if Clara is willing to be included, and she nods, too—"if you help us to get custody of your baby."

She looks around the room at all of us, as if she can't believe what we are saying. I wonder if she's going to start crying any second.

Instead she says, "I know this will probably sound crazy to you, but . . . do you think there's any way I could get a job in here?"

CHAPTER 19

CLARA

You talk about a girl with a look to drive my customers right back out into the street, this was her. With that butch haircut she look almost like a man. Look like she handed the razor to a trippin' speedfreak. Might as well shave her head she gonna go that far. Lord only knows what that new color supposed to be.

She can't look me in the eye, even askin' for a job. It ain't the first time someone off the street ask me this, but first time one who dropped a baby on me did.

"I can cook a little bit, and I've waited tables."

Days like this, I remember how far down I've been from time to time. I ain't never been low enough to throw away my babies, but I've needed help now and then. Sometimes I got it and sometimes I didn't. I try to help out other folks whenever I can.

"You got to pass a test and get a permit to work in the kitchen, honey. But if you can wait tables, I guess we can find a few hours for you."

Alicia lookin' at me now. I know she can't afford to have her own hours cut none or lose no income, but she smilin' at me like it's Christmas morning and she just opened up her bestest present. Girl got a heart of gold. I just hope this mean old world don't break it in two.

Later I find out Alicia invited Morgan to share her bedroom at Martha's house until she can get a place of her own. It figures: she homeless before, baby-daddy in and out of jail, she in and out of jail herself, that's how come she dumped her baby on us.

That don't make it right, of course, but maybe make it a little easier to understand. I've been broke, I've been hungry, I've been homeless. It can happen to anyone. I don't judge nobody. Maybe your man got money for a bottle or a baggie but none to feed the kids he gave you. One minute you healthy and happy, fat and sassy, then the next you out on the street, worried sick about where the next meal comin' from, and where you and those poor kids gonna spend the night.

All these homeless we got now, it's the worst I've ever seen. I got people comin' into my café all day long beggin' for a meal, goin' through my trash five minutes after I put it out—fightin' over who got there first and who gets to keep what I'm tossin' out—and hasslin' my customers for small bills and loose change, drivin' some of 'em away before they even come inside. We got the economy goin' like gangbusters, corporations gettin' richer every minute, unemployment supposed to be down to nothin'—how come we got all these homeless, too?

I help as many of 'em as I can, but you got to draw the line somewhere. They'd eat me right out of business if I let 'em. Lord knows I barely make enough to get by out of this café as it is. I ain't no dotcom billionaire, and I ain't got no team of lawyers and accountants figurin' out how to park my profits in Switzerland and skip out on my tax bill. Accordin' to the TV, I paid more income tax than Donald Dump did last year. He supposed to lost a billion dollars. Now that's the kind of track record you want from your business-expert President. I wasn't no great fan of Hillary Clinton's—why she stayed with that lyin', cheatin', big-nose, loser husband of hers I never will understand—but we would've been a lot better off with her than the fool we got From Russia with Love. Matter of fact, America'd been better off electing *me* President. You want to see how to run a business, you swing by here anytime. I ain't made no fortune, but I ain't never lost a billion dollars neither.

You want to know how to make America great again, Donald Dump? Here's what you do: you take the elevator up to the top of one of them fancy towers you built—or suckered somebody

else into building for you before you stiffed them on their bill—
and you open up a window in the penthouse and then just step
off, flap your wings, and see if you can fly. Go on, give it a try.
Maybe that fake hair of yours will hold you up for a while. When
you come down, try to land on one of those dodos you appointed
to take care of the environment by minin' more coal or shootin'
more elephants, kill two birdbrains with one stone if you can.
Now that's what I call a plan. Just thinkin' about it, I feel better
about America already.

Feelin' okay about myself, too, and this chance I'm takin'.
We'll see how Miss Morgan does with this new job I'm givin'
her. Between that and the free room she gettin', maybe the state
folks will let her have another chance with her baby. She can
spend some time with her and earn some money to help take
care of her. Ain't no guarantees in this world, but at least she got
a shot to turn her life around now—and her baby might got her
mama back, too.

Easy enough to turn your back on them that got it worse
than you. If nothin' else, I'll sleep good tonight knowin' I tried
to help.

CHAPTER 20

MARTHA

I was so thrilled when Alicia brought Morgan home with her to live with us. I never believed Morgan didn't really want to take care of her baby, she just needed another chance, and some help, and now she will get both. Grandma Vi says Morgan can come to church with us and meet Pastor Greg and all of our fellow worshippers there. All of the good things that have happened for me since I was saved can happen for her, too.

When I saw how skinny she is and how tired she looks, I really felt bad for her. She admitted she's been using drugs for a long time. That will have to stop right away, of course, one of Grandma Vi's rules is no drugs in this house. She even tries to get Grandpa Jack not to drink alcohol in the garage. She hasn't quite won that battle yet, but I'll bet she will. Jesus doesn't give up on anyone, neither does Grandma Vi!

Maybe you think I'm crazy for believing in second chances for someone who used drugs and abandoned her baby, but it's not like Morgan's the first person who ever made a mistake. I already told about the drugs I took, that's not the worst thing I ever did, either.

When I was fourteen and on the streets and really, really hungry one night, I let these two men fuck me in their car for a bucket of Kentucky Fried Chicken. At least it was supposed to be a bucket—they only gave me two pieces, a drumstick and a wing. They scarfed down the rest themselves, then kicked me out of the car. They said they'd kill me if I ever told anyone what we did. They said *I'd* be the bucket of chicken next time, they'd roast me over an open fire and eat the flesh right off my bones. I didn't tell anyone.

That was the first time I had sex, it was horrible, it hurt so bad. Of course, like everybody else, growing up I'd seen all these movies and TV shows making it seem like making love is the greatest thing in the world, but I didn't feel anything anywhere close to pleasure, not even for one second. As soon as it started, I just wanted it to be over. For the longest time after that, I never wanted a man to touch me ever again, I didn't get what the big deal about sex, at least for women, is supposed to be. I still don't, really, even though there were times after that when I let other men do what they wanted.

The worst part was I got pregnant. When I figured out what had happened, I came home and asked Grandma Vi to help me get rid of the baby. I didn't tell her who the men were who did it, I just said I'd been raped. I guess that wasn't exactly true since I told them they could do it, although other people have told me it was legally rape because I was so young. But Grandma Vi said if I was pregnant it was God's will, and I would just have to have the baby. I wasn't saved yet then, and I didn't believe her, so I stole some money from her and found a guy who helped me get to a clinic where they did the procedure. It just so happened that I had it done on the same day I turned fifteen. Some girls get a party for their birthday, I got an abortion.

I always wondered what kind of mother I would have been. My own mother wasn't too good at it, that's for sure. She could be sweet and loving one minute, singing me silly songs and bouncing me on her lap and tickling me, then the next minute, if some guy came over, she'd act like I wasn't even there. I don't think she ever really wanted me or understood why God gave me to her, it seemed like I was just an accident that happened to her. She never really paid much attention to me when I was starting school or tried to help me with my homework or anything, she always wanted to go out and party and leave all the work of raising a kid to Grandma Vi.

There's a lot of mothers like that, if you ask me. I see them all the time, almost everywhere I go. At church it's different, the mothers there, you can tell they really care, but just about everywhere else, you see all kinds of women who act like they should never have had kids in the first place, it sort of makes you wonder why God picks them to give babies to.

With fathers you kind of expect it, after all, they're men and they probably didn't really want to have kids anyway, or at least they don't want to be bothered with taking care of them, but mothers—I mean, why even *have* the kids if you're just going to ignore them or abuse them? One thing I absolutely cannot stand is hearing mothers yell at their little kids. The other day I was at Target and this woman leaned right into the face of this two or three year-old riding in the shopping cart and just screamed bloody murder at the little guy. You know what his big crime was? He dropped his popsicle on the floor. I almost said something to her, I really did, I sure wanted to. I wanted to tell her that's no way to teach her child how to communicate. In Psychology class we talk about this stuff all the time. Little kids are like sponges, they soak up everything they hear and see, and you can just bet that little boy will grow up remembering being screamed at like that. He started to cry, and I could tell she wanted to hit him then, instead she grabbed his little arm and shook him really hard, it just made him cry louder. It really made me sick to see that. If she had hit him, I would have said something for sure, then maybe she would have tried to hit *me*!

Grandpa Jack always says we should just stay out of other people's business. He says the world is full of fuck-ups, and we can't do anything to change that, but Grandma Vi says sometimes the Lord wants you to step in and do His work, like we're doing now by helping Morgan. We're giving her a chance to be the good mother that God wants her to be. I can't wait to help with her baby, maybe she's sort of a second chance for me, too. Like Grandma Vi says, it's all part of God's plan for our lives.

CHAPTER 21

EDUARDO

I'm the one picked to make sure that Martha's grandfather doesn't mess things up with Ms. Robinson's second home visit. I don't mind drawing this duty: I always look forward to talking with other veterans. It's sort of like what they say about going to a soccer match: you always see something you'd never seen before. When you talk to a vet, especially one who saw combat, you always learn something new, too. I might even write a book someday about the stuff I've learned from my conversations, especially if I go for history. I just read one called *Heroes from the Barrio* about Latinos in World War II. I'd love to write a book like that about the barrio guys who served with me in the Middle East, or the ones who fought in Vietnam with my grandpa or the Gulf with my dad.

I figure it's best to get Jack completely away from the house, so when Alicia and Martha introduce me to him, I ask if he has ever visited the Veterans Resource Center on the college campus. I've gotten a ton of help there and met all kinds of great people, including several who served in Vietnam like Jack. He doesn't seem too excited about it, so I throw in an offer to buy him lunch first. He isn't interested in cafeteria chow or a dry venue, so I decide to splurge on Red Robin, only to find when we get there that it has closed, another high-end chain restaurant that couldn't make it in our low-end town. I'd love to meet the marketing genius who decided to put a fifteen-dollar burger palace across the street from a community college. If they'd put in an In-N-Out instead, there'd be cars lined up around the block all day and half the night. They'd be making buckets of money, and a bunch of kids would have halfway decent part-time jobs two minutes away from their classes.

We wind up at Fat City Brew & BBQ. Two beers and a rib sandwich loosen Jack up enough to do some talking.

A lot of vets do not like to talk about what they went through, especially to civilians who can't possibly relate, but sometimes one vet will confide in another stuff that he won't share with others. I don't know if Jack cares or wants to know about my war, but I'm willing to go first if he wants me to. It turns out that he has a question.

"They let you engage over there when you had the chance, or hold you back?"

The question doesn't surprise me. Almost any Vietnam vet you talk to will tell you that the government didn't let them win a war they were capable of winning: afraid of bringing the big dog China into the fight, like in Korea.

"A little of both," I say. "Most of our jobs went according to plan. A few times we fired away and found out later that our intel was wrong, and we killed more families than targets. Other times we held our fire, and the Taliban butchered the civilians or abducted them, especially the young women. Once or twice we didn't have the transport or the ammo we needed to finish a job."

He nods. "Same old clusterfuck. The goddam politicians in bed with the corporations. Signing all those spending bills, then giving shit equipment to soldiers, ripping off the good stuff to sell to fucking Arabs, and pocketing the profits. While guys like us are getting shot to shit. Where'd you get hit?"

I tell him, as I had told Alicia, about hitting the IED outside of Ghazni. "There was a team that went in ahead of us to clear the mines, but . . . they missed a lot of other shit. Amazing what the hadjis can turn into a bomb."

Jack nods again. "Same with the gooks. Those fuckers could steal a roll of toilet paper and find a way to kill you with it. What happened?"

"My Humvee blew up and turned over. Two guys died right

away, got their skulls crushed. I was one of the lucky ones who got out alive. The medics saved my ass. Those guys are the real heroes of that war."

"Every war. The gooks knew it, too. Used to pick ours off right away, whenever they could spot 'em."

I ask if he saw the movie *Platoon* and whether it was an accurate reflection of his own experience. I mention that I watched it myself probably half a dozen times before I went into the Army. Movies have always been a big part of my life. It seems stupid to say it, considering how unrealistic most of them are, but I can't deny they were even a part of my motivation to enlist. I must have watched practically every war movie ever made with my grandfather. He thinks *Platoon* is one of the most authentic.

"I saw it," Jack says. "Once was enough for me."

"Did you see any fragging?"

"Didn't happen in my unit, but it could have. We had a few gung-ho officers who got themselves clocked by the gooks before we got the chance. There were some niggers in our Company B who would've been more than happy to put a spare round up the asshole of any glory boy takin' extra chances with their lives. Third generation West Point shitheads, trying to get themselves promoted by volunteering to get our asses killed."

"I'm *fourth* generation military myself, at least," I point out.

He grins. "Yeah, but not West Point, I'm guessing." Then he adds, "Movies get a lot of shit wrong. The one I saw came closest to getting it right was *We Were Soldiers*."

I tell him that my grandfather fought at Ia Drang. I'd read Colonel Hal Moore's book about that battle after watching the movie.

It's more than fifteen years since Jack saw it himself, and almost fifty since he was in combat, but it's all as fresh as yesterday in his mind. "That scene when Moore calls in a napalm strike? The pilot flies in too close to our lines, and a bunch of our guys get fried. Then they lift a soldier onto a stretcher, and the guy's skin comes off in another guy's hands. That's real. It happened to me. I still think about what it felt like to have that guy's flesh burning in my hands. I found out later the poor bastard lost both of his legs. He ate his gun a few years later. That could just as easy have been me. I was lucky, too, like you."

I nod and give him time to see if he wants to say more. After a moment he continues: "Another time I was lucky was when I was hiding on the floor of the jungle after our patrol got ambushed and overrun. I dug a pit for myself and covered myself with leaves and shit. A gook stepped right on top of my hand but didn't realize I was there. He finds me, either I'm chopped to pieces on the spot or shipped off to rot at Hŏa Lò."

The Hanoi Hilton, I recall, where John McCain and others were tortured. I think about telling Jack about my grandfather's work with other veterans, the support group he continues to participate in, and the soldiers he and my dad have hired to work at our nursery. I wonder if Jack would fit in with them and find their company therapeutic. Maybe he could even use the job. The only thing that stops me is his use of the *n*-word earlier. I wonder how he will refer to me when I'm out of range, if I become the *beaner* or the *wetback* he wasted some time with, and if he'd refer to my grandfather in the same way. I hold off, because my grandfather has endured enough of that shit in his lifetime, and he doesn't need to hear any more of it now.

I'll admit to a double standard here: I don't react the same way when Jack says *gook* when he's talking about guys who were trying to kill him, just like my great-grandfather's generation brought home *japs* and *krauts* from World War II—and just like me and my guys say *hadjis*. I also admit that when I'm with my friends, we call each other names that we don't want to hear from other people—sometimes, for example, they call me *blanco* just because I don't speak Spanish. Same way black guys throw the *n*-word around with each other, but they don't want to hear it from anybody else. Jack's using the word about guys who fought alongside him. I don't think any white man should use it.

I wouldn't mind if black people stopped using it, too. We'd need a whole new language for our music, that's for sure. I guess it wouldn't kill us to give up *gooks* and *hadjis* and *blanco*, too.

I ask Jack another question about the missions he served on. He wants to talk about someone else instead. He asks me if I've heard of Richard Pittman.

"Sure," I say. "They named a school after him here in Stockton. He won the Medal of Honor, right?"

Jack nods. "You know what he did to get it?"

"I've seen a few newspaper articles about him, but . . . maybe you could remind me."

"Just outside the DMZ. Took on thirty or forty gooks who had mortars, two machine guns. Fired his own until it jammed, then picked up a pistol off a dead guy and went after 'em with that and a grenade he had. A whole bunch of our wounded would've died that day, hadn't been for him. After the war, he spent the rest of his life helping other vets. That's the kind of guy they should be makin' movies about, not some asshole that got snuffed by his own crew. Too late now, though, to do Richard any good. He'd never get to see it. He died a few years ago."

"Did you know him well?"

"I knew him," he says. That's all he seems to want to say. I think about DeShaun and other guys I served with who are gone and how much it hurt to lose them.

I tell him a little more about the duty I drew before I was injured and sent home. Not that there was all that much to tell. He listens, though, and doesn't seem to mind that it was mostly nothing you would put into a movie.

"I'll bet you just tried to do your job and stay alive." He drains the last of his beer and then adds, "Just like you're doing your job right now."

"What do you mean?"

"That black gal from the government is back at Vi's house right now, ain't she?"

I nod. No point in denying it. I notice that he doesn't use the *n*-word for her and wonder what makes the difference.

"Your job was to keep the crazy old Vietnam vet from queering the deal, right? Mission accomplished, buddy. Fuck the Veterans Center. I've had enough war stories for one day. Let's go find out how our baby-savers did. They win this round, they'll probably turn the place into a goddam banana republic daycare center."

CHAPTER 22

NATALIE

Every case you work on is different and challenging in its own way. This one has a twist I hadn't run into before. I've worked many cases in which wayward mothers changed their ways, or tried to, and came back to claim children who had been taken away from them by the courts. I can't say that the track record is too encouraging. Too many of them seem to find the path back to the drugs and/or the unstable or violent men that created their problems—and problems for their kids—in the first place. I had *not* worked a case before in which a mother physically abandoned a baby and then joined the unrelated family trying to rescue her.

I am relieved to see that Jack Mackey is not sitting sentry when I arrive this time. Figuring out just how to factor him into my final report remains another complication. The immediate task, though, is to ascertain whether the circumstances in Violet Mackey's home will be conducive to raising an infant and will provide a reasonable chance for this one to thrive. I'll admit I'm feeling skeptical, based on my prior visit and what I'd learned about the birth mother since, when I ring the doorbell.

The household is ready for me this time. The whole event strikes me as almost choreographed to make the best possible impression. Morgan Welsh turns out to be contrite and apparently committed to turning her life around and sharing in the care of her baby, whom she has named Brianna. All of the other women in the house appear to be genuinely supportive. Violet Mackey and Martha Shriver in particular emphasize the support system that the church they attend will be providing to amplify the care given to the child and to her mother. I also note the positive step that Morgan has taken in securing a job at the restaurant where Alicia Gonzales works. I visit the room where Brianna would be staying with Morgan and Alicia if I permit her to be brought here. The room is small and the conditions will be cramped, to say the least, but it is very clean and hardly the worst place I have inspected where a baby would be cared for.

At the end of the visit I have some news to give them: "There is a complication with the medical report."

The doctor who examined Brianna at the county hospital found preliminary evidence of possible chromosome damage, probably from Morgan's usage of alcohol, cocaine, and/or methamphetamine during her pregnancy. I explain this as non-judgmentally as possible. Again, this is hardly the first case I'd worked in which this condition has surfaced. Morgan's head goes down and stays there.

"It's possible that Brianna will face . . . significant obstacles in mastering basic skills. Before we can proceed with the request to place her here, we need to be sure that the care-givers are prepared to deal with the challenges that may come with her condition."

"These girls help me every day," Violet says right away. "It's not easy living in this chair, but I manage because of all the help they give me."

"I appreciate your sharing that, Mrs. Mackey, and I'm glad you are getting the support that you need. All of you need to understand that the needs of an infant, especially one who may have medical issues, are different even from those of adults with physical limitations."

They take turns assuring me of their willingness to do whatever is necessary, Morgan having less, and Tori Maxwell more, to say on this score than any of the others. I move to wrap things up, still wondering how Morgan took that almost inconceivable step of leaving her baby on the restroom floor. Alicia, conversely, is perhaps the most earnest and impressive prospective adoptive mother I have ever met. My heart goes out to her. I wonder, will her compassion and intelligence be enough to offset the birth mother's capriciousness?

As I'm almost out the door, Martha jumps out of her chair, takes my arm, and walks—really, almost carries—me out to my car. She's talking a mile a minute, and I'm trying to track her message while finding my keys in the jumble of my purse. Suddenly she's crying and confessing something I would hardly have expected to hear from a member of a family seeking custody of an infant. She tells me about the tragedy she went through as an early teen and begs me to help her get the chance to redeem herself. I get the feeling that she thinks she's bound for eternal damnation if I fail to comply. I wonder how much of this her grandmother and her pastor have put into her head.

A confession: I am agnostic. I respect everyone's right to believe as they wish, and I appreciate the support that many religious organizations supply to those in need, but I have seen for myself no convincing evidence of an active (nor certainly of a benevolent) supreme being directing our lives. I am willing to hold out the hope for a better life to come, but to base our lives in the here and now upon this hope seems wishful at best and wasteful at worst. I say none of this to Martha, of course, nor do I tell her of another matter in which our paths are more similar.

When I was eighteen and a freshman at Berkeley, I went to a rave with a group of my casual friends that included several boys. We all had too much to drink or smoke, and when we got back to our dormitory, one of the boys on the football team whom I knew only slightly offered to escort me back to my room. He was a BMOC who could (and, as I later learned, *did*) have any woman he wanted, so of course I was flattered that he was paying attention to someone ordinary-looking like me. My roommate was away at her parents' home for the weekend, so no one else was there. He got my clothes off without too much of a fight, and we had unprotected intercourse. It lasted for about five minutes, as I recall. He came inside me and then got up and left.

I make no excuses for myself: it wasn't easy getting into UC Berkeley from an Oakland high school, ten minutes away, with my unspectacular SATs, but I had earned very good grades, including an A in Human Biology. I knew the facts of life, yet I behaved like an idiot. This was not too long after the height of the AIDS crisis, and truly terrible things could have happened to me as a consequence. What did happen was that I got pregnant.

The hardest part of the ensuing ordeal was telling my parents, knowing they were going to be almost as disappointed with me as I was with myself, especially since I was just getting started at Berkeley, and they had been so proud of me for getting in. My mother wanted me to give birth and even offered to raise the baby as her own, as so many grandmothers have done and continue to do. This, of course, would have meant for me more of a much younger brother or sister than a child of my own. When it comes to family matters, my dad usually takes his cues from my mother, but he surprised me this time. He said it was my body and my decision, and he would support whatever choice I made. He wound up driving me to the clinic for the procedure, paying for it, and then bringing me home until I could pull myself together. He even took a few days off from work to sit by my bedside, holding my hand, until I could muster the strength to crawl out from under the covers and face the world again. I'll never forget the long, hard hug he gave me when he dropped me off back at my dormitory, or the words he said to me then:

"Sometimes the hardest person to forgive is yourself. I know you have the strength within you to put this behind you and move forward."

He was right about that. Those first few torturous days afterward notwithstanding, I have never regretted the decision. I was not remotely prepared to take on the responsibility of having a child, and I was just at the beginning of the opportunity to earn a world-class education and to make for myself a life of far more fulfillment and accomplishment than had been available to my parents. I had no meaningful relationship with the boy who would have been the child's father, and of course no indication that he would ever have been prepared to share in the responsibility of providing for the product of his brief amusement. I thought about him when I heard Brett (or should I say Bart?) Kavanaugh testifying about his high school days. And now Kavanaugh has joined Anita Hill's abuser Clarence Thomas on the Supreme Court, where these men have the power to prevent other women from taking the step I took to salvage my own future.

I came of age in the era when the sanctity of Roe v. Wade was an article of faith among educated people in this country. I have dedicated my career to helping others, and especially other women, to make informed decisions about their lives and their families. This seems to me more important than ever now, with a new generation of conservatives thrusting their religious beliefs into our laws, opposing sex education and birth control at the front end of the reproductive cycle and termination of pregnancy at the other, in some cases even when rape or incest has taken place. To have the freedom to control our own bodies now under serious threat from the mostly men in Congress, who face none of the consequences of their legislative efforts, men who want to defund Planned Parenthood while spending more and more on prisons to house the ultimate products of *un*planned pregnancies, is truly one of the most illogical and alarming developments in my lifetime.

As I'm standing here trying to comfort fellow-traveler Martha, a car pulls up with Jack Mackey in the passenger seat. I can't help wondering if he has been conveniently extracted from his foxhole for the duration of my interview. I think back to his comment, not the first time I'd heard it, that I had no business supervising placement of children without having raised children of my own. The truth is, in some ways I never put the Berkeley incident completely behind me. To be treated that way by a man left its mark. I've had my share of relationships since, several long-term, tried living-with a couple of times, even contemplated marriage, but I never found a man that I trusted completely to be committed to fatherhood. To bring a life into this world without a committed partner to share in the journey—that's the mistake I've tried to steer other women away from.

Now we have some extremists among the feminists proclaiming that women can do a better job of raising their kids by themselves, that all they need from a man is the semen, that most men actually harm children more than they help them because they are so inept as fathers. I don't believe it, though. I consider myself a feminist, too, but I still believe that children need their fathers. I certainly needed mine. I see that the driver in the car with Jack is Alicia's friend Eduardo, and I wonder if he is prepared to be the man in this house if I allow a baby to come aboard.

Again, I don't say any of this to Martha, who would probably just consign me to hell right along with her anyway, for the cohabitations if not for the abortion. I need to get out of here before Jack can seize the opportunity to interrogate me again. I put my arm around Martha and tell her I'll do the best I can to write a fair report.

She nods, sniffles, and finally stops crying.

"We'll leave it in God's hands, then."

PART II: THE CIRCLE OF DUTY

"If you pick up a starving dog and make him prosperous, he will not bite you. This is the principal difference between a dog and a man."

> —Mark Twain, *Pudd'nhead Wilson's Calendar,* from *Pudd'nhead Wilson and Those Extraordinary Twins*

"I thought it best to be as useful as I could, and to render what kind services I could, to those immediately about me; and to try to let that circle of duty gradually and naturally expand itself."

> —Esther Summerson, in Charles Dickens' *Bleak House*

"Our first duty consists in overcoming our self-centeredness— to inconvenience oneself, to deprive oneself—when one of our human brethren is in danger, whoever he may be, from wherever he may come."

> —Jeanne Brousse, Righteous Among the Nations for helping to save Jewish families in Annecy, France during World War II, quoted by Mordecai Paldiel

"I see no shame in the failure to achieve but only in the failure to attempt."

> —Malcolm Wade, *Lost Causes and Last Calls of a Forgotten Pedagog*

CHAPTER 23

EDUARDO

I guess that movie will just have to wait.

Alicia phones me about half an hour before I'm supposed to pick her up. She asks if I'd like to meet Brianna. For a second the name doesn't register, but then, of course, I remember. It turns out that Ms. Robinson has authorized a trial period at Martha's grandmother's house, and the baby has just arrived.

As soon as I get there, I can tell we won't be making it to any movie theater. Alicia is in love—and not with me. Or at least not with me in the way she's in love with this baby.

Morgan is at the café, putting in some of the hours that Alicia gave up to help her out. Even though money is tight for her, I can tell it was a trade Alicia would make any day of the week. I don't think I've ever seen anyone as happy as she is to hold and cuddle that baby. She's going to make a fabulous mother, that's for sure. It's hard not to wonder how she'll keep going with school and work and taking care of a newborn, but she says she's going to get a lot of help.

I'm not so sure about that. Tori and Moua are happy about the baby and all, but I don't sense from either of them the connection that Alicia has. Maybe that's just because she's the one who found her and started the whole process of bringing her here. Tori actually seems kind of upset, almost jealous maybe, as if Alicia is monopolizing the baby. When Tori tries to hold her for a while, Brianna keeps trying to move her head so she can keep her eyes on Alicia. When she can't see her, she starts crying. Tori hands her back over pretty quick. Moua doesn't seem that keen to hold the baby. Maybe she's already had her turn. When Alicia asks me if I want to, of course I say "sure." What else are you going to say?

I have four younger brothers, so holding a little one is nothing new to me. I know how to keep the head steady and make eye contact and rock them a little bit and all that basic shit. I changed diapers and prepared bottles and wiped up vomit and helped my mom with all the other stuff that goes with babies. A lot of guys who grow up in Mexican families don't do that because their sisters handle it, but we were all boys in my family until my mom finally hit the jackpot and got her baby girl, number six. By then I was in high school and busy with sports, so my brothers got the duty with her.

I see Brianna twisting again to see Alicia, so I turn my body to make it easy for her. I don't want the tears on my watch that Tori got on hers. Tori seems a little upset with me, too, like how come I know how to do this and she doesn't? Moua sees the tension on Tori's face and kind of cracks a little smile, and I figure out right then that they aren't exactly best friends forever. I hope Brianna never gets stranded in no-man's-land between these two.

Martha pushes her grandmother in through the front door. They've come back from their church, where they've been holding a little fund-raiser on Brianna's behalf. Their attitudes are a little more reassuring. Martha's all smiles when she reports the meeting's results: a nice little kick-start for Brianna's college fund. I pay a little more attention to the grandmother this time. I look to see if I can find any trace in her face of the woman that a young Jack Mackey fell in love with a half-century or so ago. I can't really tell if she was ever pretty. Mostly she seems really tired. It's clear that living in the wheelchair has taken its toll on her, but her eyes light up when I hand her the baby. Alicia walks around behind the chair to stay in Brianna's line of sight while Violet holds her and coos at her. I move over to stand next to Alicia and take in the view. It all makes me remember how each successive baby in my family became the center of our world for a while, and then when mom finally got the girl she always wanted, the center of the universe.

Alicia whispers to ask if I'm mad about the movie. I just smile at her. Who needs a movie when you can hold a baby instead?

We finally get a few minutes alone together—or as alone as you can be in a medium-sized house with four other women and a baby—on the front room couch after Brianna goes down for a nap. For a long time we just sit there, content to be together, and I realize that neither of us feels the need to fill the silence with chatter. It's a good feeling. A few girls I've gone out with were always saying things like "Tell me what you're thinking" every time there was a lull in the conversation, and I never got comfortable with that pressure. Of course, let's be honest, as a guy, a lot of times what I was thinking was some variation of *What do I have to do to get this girl into my bed?* It was always a challenge figuring out how to work *that* into the conversation. For some reason now, even though I'm more attracted to Alicia than to any woman I've ever been with, I don't feel any urgency to take this to the next level. I feel like it's going to happen when the time is right, and in the meantime I just want to enjoy being with her.

Eventually, she tells me a little more about her new schedule and how Brianna will fit into it. I tell her I hope I will fit into it, too.

"I'm sure you will. You did very well holding her today."

"Next time maybe I can show off my diapering technique."

"I can hardly wait to see that. Maybe we'll sell tickets."

"Good idea. More money for that college fund."

She has a night shift to get to at Clara's café, so I don't stay too long. When she walks me to the door to say goodbye, she smiles into my eyes and tilts her head up, and I realize that she wants me to kiss her. I have been known to miss this signal in the past, but not this time. I give her what she wants, taking it soft and slow, knowing it's what I want, too.

On my way out, I see Sergeant Mackey watching from a chair in front of the garage. I go over to say hello.

"Want some free advice?"

"Sure. Always willing to learn from a man of your experience."

"From the looks of that goodbye smooch, you're on the fast track to Fucked City, my friend. Here's my advice: if the word *marriage* enters your mind, or hers, run like hell. Go back to the Army if you have to. Shit, go back to Afghanistan, as fast as you can. Anything's better than *that*. If you get married, you might as well just cut off your cock and balls and hand 'em over to her to keep in her purse, next to her collection of credit cards, to be taken out only when the mood strikes her. I guarantee you, she'll be pulling out the credit cards a lot more often than your pecker. And if she does let you touch her, the babies start coming, and you spend the next twenty years cleaning up whatever messes they make of their lives—and yours. Then, just when you think that's about over and you might have a goddam minute or two for yourself, your kid has a kid and the whole fuckin' rigamarole starts all over again." He pauses for second. "Just thought I should warn you what you're gettin' into."

"It was one kiss," I say. "Our first, actually. I don't think we'll be sending out the wedding invitations any time soon." Even as I say these words, I feel a tiny trace of annoyance at myself, as if I have somehow betrayed Alicia. And I realize that, yes, this is a woman that I could see myself marrying, *wanting* to marry. It's the first time I've felt that way.

"Just don't send one to me, okay? I've had enough marriage, my own and every other one I've seen or smelled, to last me a lifetime."

I move to redeem myself, with results more far-flung than I could ever have anticipated. "No promises, Jack. If I decide to marry this girl, and she decides to marry me, I think we'll both want you at the ceremony. You're a member of this family."

"Bullshit. I'm the crazy old coot who shits in the park, remember?"

On a day that began with a new movie that I missed, I flash for some reason to a scene from a golden-oldie, one of my grandfather's all-time favorites, which I must have sat and watched with him at least twenty times: *Rio Bravo,* when John Wayne's Chance expresses his affection for Walter Brennan's Stumpy. I snatch Jack's cap off and plant a quick kiss on top of his head.

It's a perfect way to end the most romantic evening of my life so far.

CHAPTER 24

MOUA

So Tori knocks on my door and tells me her latest walking penis wants a three-way and am I up for it? I tell her to go down the hall and see if Martha and the g-ma are interested, make it a foursome instead. They can snap a few photos to sell to *Ripley's* or *National Geographic* while they're at it.

I'm thinking that will get rid of her, but she steps past me and comes into my room, without being invited. She's got one of her super-scoop tops on and her assets on full display, as usual.

"You know how you can tell if a man really loves you?"

Alicia isn't home from work yet, so I guess it's my turn to listen to the postmortem.

"I can hardly wait to find out."

"Smart ass. You should listen up and learn something. Maybe even take notes, in case you ever grow out of that Asian training bra."

She's eyeing my itty-bitties and making sure I get the point that this is something she is in a position to lecture on and I can only hope to learn from.

"Just tell him you're going to have breast reduction surgery. All you have to do is watch his face when you tell him. You can tell in a heartbeat if he gives a shit about all the pain you'll go through in the surgery or the relief you'll feel from not having to carry around your twins all day—or if all he cares about is the prime nookie he'll be missin' out on after."

"So how did your date—what's his name? Morris?—do on the test?"

"Maurice. Flunked it. Looks at me like I just told him his Mama backed over his dog and then went off a cliff, in his brand new Benz. I'm just messin' with him, of course. No way I'm givin' up on my girls"—she cups herself with both hands, her subtle way of making sure I don't miss the point—"but I can tell he's an asshole."

"*All men are assholes*. You told me before. You told Alicia, too."

"Still true."

"Why do you go out with them, then? With anyone who asks, I mean?"

"Are you tryin' to say I have low standards?"

"Of course not. I'd never say that about you. I'm saying you have *no* standards."

"You lookin' to get your ass kicked tonight, ain't you?"

"Sorry. I couldn't resist. Were you finished, or is there more you wanted to—?"

"Then we had the sex talk. You know, just to be clear he don't have no fatal diseases or nothin', or six babies with his home girls. You know what that fool said to me?"

You never know what the kind of guys Tori goes out with might say to her face to try to impress her, although I probably could make an educated guess based on some of the stuff I hear on the phone.

"He start talkin' 'bout some bro he know claim he got fifteen kids by twelve different girls. I say to him, 'Why the fuck you tellin' this to me?' Pimp daddy like that, go around droppin' babies right and left and braggin' about it, they ought to lock him up for the rest of his life, and cut off his dick for good measure. Can you imagine what those girls he got with must go through to get any child support out of that nigga? Shit, you might as well try to get milk from his asshole."

"We seem to keep coming back to that term. So Maurice is definitely—"

"You know what else he say to me? Get this: he smile real sexy and say, 'Anal is the new oral.' You believe that shit?"

It's not the first time I've heard it, but I shake my head.

"I say back to him, 'Well, you talkin' to a old-fashioned girl here. And you ain't gettin' so much as a kiss on the cheek out of me unless you start showin' a little respect. You sure as hell ain't gettin' no blowjob on the first date, and you even think about stickin' it in my backdoor, you better run for cover and you better run fast, because I be blastin' your pretty face with pepper spray like you a damn raccoon in the backyard trash. Then my big brother, the one who played football'—I made that shit up, but they always believe it—'gonna get all medieval on *your* ass with a baseball bat'—I guess big brother play baseball, too—'take a big swing at your little dick, teach you where to stick it and where not to, if you get my drift.'"

"Did he?"

"Did he what?"

"Get your drift. Or did you have to pepper spray him? I thought you told Alicia you were upgrading to Mace anyway."

"Forget that weak-ass shit. Gettin' me a Taser before I go out with that fool again."

I try to be helpful. "Maybe you should try going out with a woman instead."

She laughs. "That your plan? Marry another woman, then? What you gonna do for dick? Strap it on?"

"I didn't say anything about marrying anyone."

"'Course, most women are assholes, too. Bitches will steal your man in a minute if they can. They'll do it even if they don't even like him, don't really want him. Just to take him away from you. Just to prove they hotter than you. Just because they can."

"No one's hotter than me," I deadpan, just because I can. "And I don't need a man that would dump me for someone like that."

"You a independent woman, that what you sayin'?"

I shrug. "I can support myself. I don't need a man—or a woman—to pay my bills. Or tell me what to do—in bed or anywhere else."

She laughs again. "Just on the phone, huh?"

"Maybe you should give it a try sometime. It's pretty lucrative."

"How much you make last month?"

I can almost see her toting up her wages and tips and preparing the put-down comparison.

"Sorry. That's classified."

"You doin' okay, though, huh? Long as Martha and Grammy don't find out how you payin' the rent, I mean."

I hear the threat behind her words. The phone rings before I can answer her.

"Sorry. I have to take this."

I hear Alicia come in and go straight to Martha's room to find Brianna. As I pick up the phone for Felix, who fantasizes about life as a tranny and wants to try on my panties, Tori waves a hand to dismiss the important work I'm doing and goes to join her there, I'm pretty sure for another rendition of the charms of Maurice.

CHAPTER 25

BOOKER

The college offered another enhanced retirement package this year to try to get the old guard like me to give up the ghost. That way, the administration can replace the classes we teach by hiring a handful of freeway flyers at a fraction of the cost in salary and no benefits. Then go out and hire more bureaucrats to explain to the public why we are graduating students who can't identify the three branches of their country's government or write a complete sentence, let alone a coherent essay, and why the degrees we are offering aren't worth the paper they're printed on. Oh, and in the meantime, please support the half-billion dollar bond measure we are floating to increase funding to our campus.

Given all this nonsense, my long-term colleagues act like I'm crazy when I tell them I have no plans to walk away. I ask them, retire and do what? Sit at home and wait for the list of honey-dos that I can't do even if I wanted to, which I damned well don't? Replace the curtain rods? Regrout the tile? How will these projects make our lives any better, any more fulfilling? I'm more likely to put a screw through my thumb than into the wall, or to inhale deadly toxins from whatever fluid I'm supposed to be scrubbing with. Even if I duck the chores, I'm stuck, just like when school's out and I'm on vacation, in the Vast Wasteland. My wife has filled her empty nest with televisions. She has one in every room: the kitchen, the living room, the family room, the bedroom, even the guest rooms. Her day starts with *Joy in the Morning*. Next come the soap operas and the *Real Housewives* reruns, and then the endless evening parade of punchless pundits on MSNBC: first Rachel and then Lawrence and then Brian, all basically doing the same show every night, night after night, delighting in TrumPutin's latest gaffe and smugly predicting the end of the regime, just like they predicted a landslide for Hillary—while the Republicans in power keep right on running the country into the sewer. I'm sorry, but Schadenfreude is not a helpful political platform. I hate the Reich as much as the next man and more than most, but what good does it do to give a public forum to a parasite like Michael Avenatti? I'd almost rather listen to the country music channel—which my wife has also been known to turn on. She must be the only black woman outside of Texarkana who can abide that yowling. Don't even get me started on the other contemporary *music* she's trying to get me to open my mind to and *learn how to appreciate*.

I admit, I'm out of touch. I am a product of the generation that produced The Beatles, and I still haven't the faintest idea what all of that excitement was about. I understand that even now people pay hundreds, even thousands of dollars, to get into a Paul McCartney concert. I wouldn't cross the street to hear that man sing for free. You could walk into any black church in America on any Sunday and easily find ten or fifteen voices vastly superior to his, and far more soulful. You wouldn't even need to hold tryouts. Mick Jagger at least *has* a voice, but of course it's his swagger, not his musicianship, that made and keeps him famous. He, anyway, showed some understanding of those who paved the way for him—unlike John Lennon. That ignoramus is most often chastised, of course, for "We're more famous than Jesus," but for a millisecond in history he may actually have been right about that. What he ought to have been crucified for was "Before Elvis there was nothing." No, Mr. Lennon: before Elvis there was Muddy Waters. Before Elvis there was Chester Burnett. Long before Elvis, there was Louis Armstrong, and there was Fats Waller. Before Elvis there was everything: you just weren't paying attention. Fortunately for Elvis, he *was* paying attention. But now we have another generation of *artists* who know nothing of these names, whose *music* is based not on years of study of the masters and dedication to their craft but on imbecilic rants and rimes backed by mindless pounding of percussions. If my wife is going to expect me to listen to *that,* I am much better off coming to work and dealing with whatever nonsense I find here.

This latest attempt to induce my retirement reminds me of what Coach Pendleton, the most vital man I've ever known, said to me when his own time came. I was still practically a kid then, just settling in here at the community college after failing to make the tenure cut at CSU for shooting my mouth off too much. It was a kind of bond between us: he had been canned at another CSU for one too many diatribes about his corrupt and incompetent Athletic Director and the gutless President who wouldn't fire *him.* Coaches don't enjoy the same protections that tenured faculty do. He'd found out the hard way that you can't count on keeping your job if you make a habit of telling your boss to pull his head out of his ass. Soon after I landed here, he befriended me when I offered to give some extra help to some of the students on his basketball team who were struggling to maintain their eligibility. He was hitting sixty-five or so—a point I'm well past now myself—and tired of losing, after back-to-back hard-luck seasons following years of sustained success. He had pushed athletes of middling talent to far greater glory than they had any right to expect, even winning a state championship, until they started tuning out his demands for all-out effort on defense and coherent shot-selection on offense. When he finally despaired of getting them to pay attention, he quit. This was back in the day when there were still two major daily newspapers coming out of San Francisco, one with an afternoon press run. After he quit, when I asked him what he was doing in retirement, he said, "Get up in the morning and wait for *The Chronicle.* Then sit around and wait for *The Examiner.*" It was a cautionary tale, to say the least, one that I have remembered across all these years—and there's no extra edition these days to fill the p.m. hours.

The other problem I would face if I retired, of course, is that there is just too damn much food in my house at all times.

If I weren't working in my office or classroom seven or eight hours a day, I'd be home with far too much temptation a few steps away all day. I'm already at least fifty pounds over my ideal weight, a far cry from where I used to be. Even though I was never an athlete, Coach Pendleton convinced me of the value of a daily workout, and I kept that up for a few years. Nothing like his own, of course: he did two hundred push-ups and five hundred sit-ups before breakfast every day, religiously, almost right up until he died. I never attempted anything on that order of madness. But at least I walked or jogged and did a few calisthenics now and then when he was around to growl at me. Those days are long gone, I'm afraid. I'm already a part of the obesity epidemic that has overtaken our country. If the elevator is out in this building, which it seems to be just about every other week, and I have to climb four flights to my office, by the time I get here I'm a candidate for a heart attack and a helicopter ride to UC Davis Medical Center. In this regard I'm hardly a role model for my students of the Hellenic ideal: *a sound mind in a sound body*. Retirement would probably push me into the Sumo wrestler category. Coach P would be ashamed of me.

I'm thinking again now about my departed old friend, a white man who went out of his way forty years ago to befriend a new black faculty member, when I hear the knock on my office door, a rarity at this stage of my career. Most of my students can barely be bothered to make it to class, let alone visit me before or after. I open the door to find Mr. Martinez, a young veteran of the War on Terror. He has written several impressive essays in my American History class. He struggles a bit with grammar and formal usage, as nearly all of today's students do, but he is working hard to improve. He is here now to ask some follow-up questions about my comments on his most recent essay.

Most of my students do not welcome criticism. They want one thing from me: a grade that will help them to achieve their goals. Most of them have very little interest in history, and many are not shy about confessing this, even to the benighted old soul charged with giving them instruction in it. A list of their priorities would look something like this:

1. Their cell phone.
2. Their Facebook account.
3. Their video games and playlists.
4. Their significant other/bother or lack thereof.
5. Their friends.
6. Their job, jobs, or lack thereof.
7. Their car, truck, or lack thereof.
8. Their clothes.
9. Their shoes.
10.-99. Other stuff.
100. My class.

Mr. Martinez, conversely, listens carefully to my suggestions, takes notes, and thanks me for correcting his errors and for noting the virtues, of which there are many, in his work. In his latest essay he has tackled the topic of America's role in the tearing down of the Berlin Wall and has offered a cogent contrast with our current President's fixations. Although he has given more credit to Ronald Reagan than I am comfortable with, I have to concede that he has constructed his argument thoughtfully, including that President's insistence, over the objections of his advisors, on including in his most iconic speech his most iconic words: "Mr. Gorbachev, tear down this wall!" I even concede that Reagan would be a vast improvement upon the generation of blowhards and toadies comprising the GOP today. I remind Mr. Martinez now, however, that Reagan also defined his legacy by opposing the Civil Rights Act of 1965.

"Thirty years ago," I tell him, "when the Berlin Wall came down, many of my friends and colleagues believed that we were at the dawn of a new era. They believed that America had at last conclusively prevailed in the war against the Evil Empire, and that we would soon find a way to export our sacred democracy to Russia and China and other autocratic societies surrounding us, changing the world in the process. George H. W. Bush and Bill Clinton should have seized the opportunity to dispatch a hundred thousand engineers and Peace Corps workers to those countries to build the bridges and bonds that might have paved the way to a world of peace and prosperity; of course, we know what Mr. Clinton was otherwise preoccupied with. Now instead we have Russia, no longer under the visionary leadership of a Gorbachev or a Yeltzin but under a killer with a KGB pedigree, as menacing as ever, meddling in our elections, purveying weaponry and war in the Middle East, threatening Europe, suppressing dissent and individual freedoms at home, and poisoning those who dare oppose them abroad. Meanwhile, China 'elects' a lifetime ruler and expands its influence all across the planet, launching vast, transformative infrastructure projects, while our own President, as you have so pertinently observed, urges us to use our resources to wall off Mexico. If my friends and colleagues had spent a little more time actually participating in the Civil Rights Movement, rather than merely admiring it from afar, their optimism might have been tempered with a bit of realism. Progress comes by inches, not by leaps and bounds, and back-sliding is pervasive."

He asks about my own Civil Rights background, one of the few students in recent memory courteous or interested enough to inquire. I tell him briefly about my own tiny role in the Movement, including marching with John Lewis when I was sixteen years old. In spite of his own military background, he does not appear to judge me, unlike some in my own family, when I tell him about declaring myself a conscientious objector to avoid service during the Vietnam War, not that this would necessarily have prevented my being conscripted against my will.

"I had an older brother who died in Vietnam. My father had served with the Tuskegee Airmen in World War II. He didn't speak to me for ten years after I declined to be drafted. He never even congratulated me on my doctoral degree. I think he was prouder of my brother for dying there than he was of me for earning a PhD."

"How did you—"

"Avoid service? I was fortunate," I tell him. "I had been

accepted as an undergraduate at the University of Toronto, so I declined a few other, more promising offers, went there in 1968 when I turned eighteen, and stayed, got started on graduate school, until Nixon gave up his brilliant plan to bomb the Viet Cong into submission and finally got us out—and we got *him* out."

"My grandfather says that war was a mess from start to finish. He served there."

"I suspect that the soldiers who do the actual fighting in any war mostly feel the same way—especially as opposed to the civilian public dependent upon journalists caught up in the wonders of *Shock and Awe*."

He nods. "I just hate it when some moron like Mark Wahlberg pops off about how, if only he'd been sent with the SEALS to get Bin Laden, they would have taken him alive. Most people have no clue what it took to pull that mission off."

"I'm sure I'm one of them. I've always been more interested in peace, but you don't earn a postgraduate degree in history without thoroughly studying war. In spite of all I've read, I know there is no way a civilian like me can learn from a book what someone like you has learned from experience."

"It's funny you say that. I've actually been thinking about writing a book about what me and my guys went through—"

He sees my raised eyebrows, stops, and corrects himself.

"Excuse me: *my guys and I—*"

I nod my approval of his self-edit.

"—went through in Afghanistan."

"The 'graveyard of empires.' Eighteen years and counting now: our longest war. Did you know that Herman Melville referenced the British Empire's 'bloody battle' there a hundred and seventy-some years ago, in *Moby-Dick*?" I smile indulgently, recalling that beastly mother of all American books, and think about the years of work that went into three of my own. "You are

certainly capable of doing that. A book is a big project, though—
and getting it published even bigger. I'd suggest that you start
with an essay."

I encourage him to revise his Berlin Wall essay and submit
it for possible publication in the campus Social Science
Department's magazine. He seems surprised but pleased that I
would suggest this. I tell him he will have to continue working
hard to clean up his grammar and style issues, but he has the
potential to be a writer if he chooses to pursue this field. I also
offer to read and critique anything he writes about his own
experiences overseas.

He thanks me and then, rather than sampling his war stories
for me, as seems opportune, he shifts the focus back to me.
"What was it like for you in Toronto?"

I can tell, without his saying so, that he wants to know if a
black man was treated better there than at home in the United
States. I remind him that I grew up in Alabama. "Any northern
city would have been an improvement for me, but Toronto was
particularly cosmopolitan. Most of the people I met there were
hospitable, even gracious. There were some places where I wasn't
welcome, even there, and some of my professors were skeptical
about my qualifications, but I managed to prove them wrong. It
wasn't always easy. As a U.S. citizen it was hard for me to get
any substantial financial aid. I took every job I could get to cover
my expenses: washing dishes, waiting tables, grading papers—
once I had established myself a bit—for professors who were
too busy with the books they were writing to pay any attention
to their students' scribblings. I imagine you, on the other hand,
are taking advantage of the G.I. Bill?"

He nods. "It covers a lot. On the weekends I help out at my
dad's nursery. He pays me a little more than he probably should.
I'm hoping to get a scholarship if I can keep my grades up. In
high school I kind of slacked off on that. I figured I was going
into the Army, so my grades didn't really matter. College was the
last thing on my mind—school was for nerds. I did just enough

studying to stay eligible for wrestling and soccer. That's all I focused on—and girls, of course. I didn't pay too much attention in my classes. I really regret it now."

"No tragedy there. You still have plenty of time to distinguish yourself academically."

He tells me then about weighing a teaching career versus pursuing nursing, his interest in history at odds with his sense of what will be a more viable path to employment and helping others. I tell him I can't advise him on that score: he will have to follow his own heart.

When he leaves, I think about all the girls I didn't kiss at his age, before and after as well, when I was ensconced in various barren garrets and carrels, and about all the sports I never attempted. How different the paths of my students' lives have been from my own, how different our regrets!

CHAPTER 26

VIOLET

I am truly blessed. The Lord works in mysterious ways His wonders to perform. I do not ask of Him why He has seen fit to confine me to this chair, nor why He has bestowed upon me and upon my family so many other trials: war, alcoholism, addiction, separation, divorce, self-destruction, fire—all of these, I know, are somehow part of His plan. Everything happens for a reason, and there is a purpose to His ways that none of us can comprehend. He took my Martha away from me, twice, as He took away her mother, and sent them forth to discover for themselves the folly of worldly ways. With the Lord's divine guidance Martha has come back to me and back to the church. She has found a new purpose in life in helping to care for my needs, along with her friends with whom we are blessed to share this house.

Now the girls have brought a baby, and the mother who abandoned her, into our home. I have welcomed both with open arms. As with the other girls whom I have taken in, their background does not matter to me. The baby's race is not important. The mother's mistakes have been forgiven. God loves all of His children equally. All that matters is the preparation for the Kingdom to come, helping to raise a child who loves the Lord and devotes her life to doing His will on this Earth as it shall be done in Heaven.

Today we shall take the first step toward baby Brianna's salvation. We shall take her to our church to be dedicated by our wonderful Pastor Greg Whitfield, the most righteous man I have ever been blessed to know.

CHAPTER 27

MORGAN

Fuck this shit. These people are fucking nuts. If this is my choice, come here every Sunday for the rest of my life or go straight to hell, I pick hell. It's not even close.

At first I wasn't gonna go, because I know I'll be the center of attention and all of these Jesus freaks will be standing around staring up my skirt like I'm the purple-assed baboon at the fucking zoo. Then I remembered about the money that Martha and Granny scored off these cuckoos for Bri, and I figure maybe there's more where that came from. Can't hurt to check it out. I put on this stupid dress that Martha gives me that's like four sizes too big for me, and I cover up what I can of my tats with a sweater, bundle up Bri, stick a pacifier in her mouth, and then follow along like a little motherless lamb when Martha and Granny drag me in to show off their latest salvage job.

As soon as they introduce me to him, Father or Pastor (or whatever the fuck he is) Greg puts his arms around me like I'm his long-lost wife that disappeared years ago on the high seas and just now somehow found my way home. He tries his best to rub against my tits, which are still swollen from the milk. I have to remember to get that damn shot to shut it off. I don't need Bri clawing at me every chance she gets to go for a mouthful. I feel his pitiful dick poking against me down below while he's studying the tats I couldn't hide up top. I'm thinking, *if this fucker says anything about he knows a guy who can remove those for a small fee, I'll say back, "I know a guy who can remove your balls, for free."* I can't get away from that creep fast enough.

Fortunately, he has to go start the program, so he and his half-ass hard-on go up to the podium and the show begins. If you're ever invited to party with the Pentecostals, I have just one piece of advice for you: *don't.*

I've never seen such bullshit in my life. Father/Pastor/Pervert Greg talks and talks until I'm starting to think about rubbing one out just to stay awake. When he finally stops, they start up this horrible music they should have saved for torturing POWs. Face it: if God wanted Christians to rap, He would have made them black. They could really use some Jay-Z or Polo G in this pit. Greg comes down into the congregation and starts urging people to say what they are feeling, and these crazy fuckers all around me start jibber-jabbering in words that don't even sound like English and don't make any fucking sense. Greg's hopping around the room touching and rubbing everybody and promising that the Lord will solve their problems and salve their wounds if they just trust in Him—and pony up to support the church, of course. When he gets to Granny's wheelchair, I'm half-expecting him to lay his hands on her and tell her by the grace of God, she's healed, she can jump right out of that chair and start twerking in the pews and babbling in pig-Latin with the rest of these Looney Tunes.

Only Martha is between him and me now, and I'm just praying he doesn't stop in front of me and put his fucking hands on me again. It turns out to be even worse: he not only stops next to me, he signals to stop the music, and then he tells the congregation about me and Bri, even though they already heard the whole fucking tale of woe from Martha and Granny last week. I close my eyes and stop myself from punching him in the face and just think about the money I'm going to get for putting up with this shit. Bri wakes up and spits out the pacifier and starts screaming her head off and won't stop, so *he* finally stops and moves on to the next victim. Granny's rocking Bri like crazy to get her to shut the fuck up, and Martha's grinning at me like we just entered Paradise and God Himself is waiting to greet us at the pearly gates with eternal salvation and hot fudge sundaes.

Except there's more bullshit to go through first. The big event is they do this stupid baby dedication ceremony for Bri up at the front of the church, with everybody crowding around to watch, like it's some big deal for Greg to lay his hand on her and declare her a child of God and act like all of her problems will suddenly disappear for the rest of her life. Bri shows her appreciation now by screaming even louder. I'm sitting there hoping she'll spit up on Greg. That would be fun to watch. I should have shaken her up a little bit before we handed her over. For once, though, she doesn't hurl, just keeps screaming through the whole deal.

When I'm thinking this bullshit is finally over, they ask me if I want to be baptized. I guess this is the big surprise they were saving for me, as if dipping me into some contaminated city tap water will solve *my* problems. Martha's beaming at me again, and Granny is raising her eyes to the ceiling like she's trying to spot The Holy Ghost hanging out up there in the rafters. Maybe she's expecting Him to pop down and perform the rest of the service personally. I really don't want Greg touching me again and pushing me under, but then I tell myself, it's just a little water. It'll dry off. And then maybe these crazy fuckers will come up with some more cash.

I let him do it. Lots of the churchies are recording it on their cell phones. They can't get enough of this shit. Fuck, they'll probably post it on their Facebook pages or put me on YouTube. Greg tries to get another free feel in, but I sort of twist out of his grip and get it over with quick. As I step away from him, I wonder if anyone has ever been kicked in the balls while performing a baptism before. Can you imagine how many YouTube hits *that* would get?

Afterward, I can't wait to get back to Granny's house and take a shower. I'm dying to wash off the holy shit water, but that fucking Tori is hogging the bathroom again. Either I have to ask to use Granny's bathroom, where the other girls deal every day with her world-famous bowel movement issues, or I have to wait. I decide to wait.

I guess I'm supposed to be saved now. You know what? Those fuckers who *saved* me are so sure it was God who gave me a baby, I just might tell them I agree. Even though I'm pretty sure it was Tyreke, not God, who was fucking me. And then I just might give goddam baby Bri back to Him. Let's see if He does any better job taking care of her than I did.

CHAPTER 28

CLARA

Maybe I can't compete with Donald Dump losing a billion dollars a year, but I lost a good six hundred out of the cash register tonight. It's not somethin' that will put me out of business, but it sure will make it harder for me to give Alicia that raise she countin' on and God knows deserves. Poor girl, barely gettin' by herself, sends home half of what I pay her to help out her family. Never should've took those hours away from her and give 'em to a mess like Morgan.

I got only myself to blame. I been in this business long enough to know better than to trust a new employee I just hired off the street to be alone with my cash. I was goin' out for maybe fifteen minutes, just long enough to drop off at the Food Bank what we didn't sell and couldn't keep for tomorrow. She been doin' so well here and at home with Alicia and them others, even got herself baptized, I just didn't think twice about leavin' her with that temptation.

When I call it in, same cops show up as before, first time Morgan was here, when she dropped her baby on us. Take my report, write down the Social Security number she give me, although she wasn't here long enough for me to cut a paycheck and find out if it's real or fake. I tell them there might be some pictures of her with the baby at the house where she stayin'. With all them tattoos she got, they don't think she'll be too hard to find. Gettin' my cash back, that's another story.

The man cop's sniffin' around here like I might got a plate of somethin' for him, even though I told him where I just got back from. Some cops eat free at my place, especially the brothers and the Mexicans and the Filipinos like his partner, although we don't got too many of those made cop in this town. I don't like this one lookin' down his nose at me, though. Don't care much for the advice he give me neither.

"A background check could come in handy next time. You might want to reconsider your hiring policies."

You might want to get your fat butt out of here and go find my money.

The lady cop gets a call and takes it outside. Man cop leans over my counter and tries to get a little friendlier. "That Mex waitress who found the baby still work here? What's her name again?"

"Her name in the report you wrote up before, I imagine. You could look it up. She got her a boyfriend now, though, not too much older than her. Combat veteran, I hear."

Lady cop stick her head in to tell him they got another call to get to. He give me a dirty look before he go. Worth it to get him gone. Of course, you got to be careful gettin' on the wrong side of cops. Maybe I'll find a worn-out burrito for him if he show up here again. I keep my kitchen clean as a whistle, but I can't control what crawls in from next-door. Not my fault if a cockroach or two climbed into it before he take a bite.

I pick up the phone to give Alicia the bad news. She got some for me, too, when she call me back.

CHAPTER 29

ALICIA

It's amazing, isn't it, how you can go from the top of the world at one minute to the very bottom in the next?

I was having one of the best days of my life. First, Eduardo calls and asks me if he can pick me up a little earlier than we had planned. He has something he wants to show me before we go to lunch and a movie. I rush to get ready, curious, of course, about what it is that he is so eager for me to see. He picks me up, and we drive for about ten or fifteen minutes to the outskirts of town. I have no idea what I'm about to see, and he's not telling me. He's just smiling and humming and seems very happy. I'm happy just to be with him. Then we pull off the road, and I see the sign: *Martinez and Sons Yard and Garden*, with big American and Mexican flags crossed beside it. It's the nursery he told me about, where he works on the weekends. He has taken the afternoon off to be with me. Morgan is covering my shift at the café.

"My grandfather started this business when he got back from Vietnam," he tells me now, as he escorts me into a courtyard where wildly colorful flowers are everywhere I turn. "He started out mowing lawns, like his father, and then he got the idea of selling his customers the plants and trees for the yards he was taking care of. I think it was therapy for him, seeing things grow, after what he had been through over there. Over the years he hired a bunch of other veterans to work here, try to help them put the war behind them. When my dad and my uncles took over the business, they kept the same tradition, giving jobs to vets from the Gulf War and Iraq and Afghanistan."

Behind a counter I see a worker with a prosthetic arm helping a customer. When he steps out from behind the counter, I see that he also has a prosthetic leg. I think again about how grateful I am never to have gone to war myself and about the challenges those who survive must face every day for the rest of their lives. And I realize that most people just talk about helping veterans who have been wounded, just look at them with pity when they see them and then forget about them five seconds later, but here is a family that is actually doing something.

"My dad bought my uncles out a few years ago. He likes to be in control rather than having to make decisions by committee. He'd love it if I took over for him someday. He thinks I'd be better off majoring in business, though, to get ready for it."

"He doesn't want you to be a nurse or a teacher?"

"He really just wants me to pick one major and stick with it, make sure that I graduate. He never got the chance to get a degree himself—too busy working to support my mom and six kids. He'll accept my choice, whatever I decide, but I know it would really make him happy if I took over here. Sometimes I think that's what I really want to do. Maybe even major in botany and learn more about all the stuff we're growing here."

"Is so beautiful here! You must find it very refreshing to come to work here."

"Most of the time that's true. Just like you, some days I have to deal with customers who are impossible to satisfy. A few people have tried to sue us after they drowned the trees they planted, or the bushes they bought from us didn't fill out overnight as much as the ones we have here. Some customers want instant paradise. They don't understand that it takes time and care to keep up a yard. They just want to stick stuff in the ground and show off to their neighbors. But those are the exceptions. Most of our customers really like what we do for them, and it's fun to hear back from them later or see the photos they bring in when they come back. You feel like you're really accomplishing something when you help someone create a beautiful garden where there used to be just dirt or concrete."

He gives me a tour of the most spectacular plants. We stop briefly in front of each one, and he tells me its name and something interesting about it, but not too much. Mostly he lets the flowers do the talking for him. He asks me their names in Spanish as we go. Some I know and some I don't. I clap my hands in pleasure when I see the tree that gives my favorite fruit, which Americans call pomegranate.

"We have two names for this one," I say. "We call the tree *el granado*, but the fruit we call *la granada*."

"Sound confusing," he says, with a smile, but he promises to bring me a tree to plant in the yard at Martha's grandmother's house. "If you're going to be there for a while, I mean. It'll be a year or two before it produces fruit."

I tell him the names of the other plants or trees I know, and he smiles and says this will help him with some of his customers. I smile back and tell him again that it's time for him to learn Spanish properly.

"Especially if you are going to fly that Mexican flag."

He nods. "My grandfather never forgot where his ancestors came from, and my dad didn't either. Some customers complain about that, too," he says, pointing at the red, white, and green, "but my father just says they are welcome to take their business somewhere else. You're right, though. It's time for me to learn the language. I want to take a trip, too, to see where some of my grandmother's family still live. It's kind of crazy: I've been to Afghanistan, but I've never been to Mexico. I went halfway around the world before I've even gone next door."

Maybe we will go there together sometime, I'm thinking, but of course I don't say it. I wonder what my parents would say about him. Mami would love him, this I already know, just for knowing so much about flowers and trees. All Papi will care about is how he treats me.

We leave the nursery, and Eduardo takes me to lunch at The Roadhouse, where it turns out Tori is our waitress. I admit I enjoy showing him off to her a little bit. She tries to flirt with him, of course, but he is really good about keeping his eyes off her *chichis* and on me instead. The food is good, though way too expensive in my opinion, compared to what Clara serves for less than half the cost. I tell him he doesn't have to leave Tori such a big tip, but he seems to want to. I guess he doesn't want me to hear any complaints later. Then, instead of the movie I thought we were finally going to get to, he drives us to the college campus, and we pass through the entrance where we first met. I wonder if he's as sentimental about that as I am. He asks me to take a walk with him.

I know the parking lots nearby are packed with buyers and sellers at the weekend flea market, crowding and bumping into each other and sometimes even getting into fights in their rush to get the best deals, but the middle of the campus is completely empty. We circle the lagoon and admire the koi fish and just talk about school and everything that is going on in our lives. When our hands brush against each other's, he reaches out to hold mine. It just seems so natural.

We find a bench to sit down on for a few minutes. He points out how much he likes the carving of Cesar Chavez that an artist and former professor at the college, Richard Rios, did for the library, and then points to a statue of a former United States President, Franklin Roosevelt—the one, Eduardo reminds me, who ordered the internment of Japanese Americans during World War II.

"We were talking about monuments in Booker Bisson's history class the other day," he says. "I looked around the room and saw the other students checking their phones or watching the clock, just itching to get out of there. Or falling asleep."

"Moua has this teacher, too. She says he's really boring. She takes a nap."

"Like me in high school. But now I find it really interesting. The professor wanted us to decide if we agree with tearing down the statues of Confederate leaders in the southern states. "

"I have no problem with that. Is easy to see why any black

person alive today would not want to honor the leaders of a movement that was based on slavery."

He nods. "Then he raised the question about the names on all of our schools here—like Washington and Jefferson, and whether we should change those, too. Those guys owned slaves, too—but they also helped found the country. Jefferson wrote the *Declaration of Independence*. Washington led us through the revolution and turned down the crown when they wanted to make him King. That guy"—he nods again at the Roosevelt statue—"led the nation through almost the end of the war. Defeating Japan and Nazi Germany at the same time wasn't exactly an easy job—and he did it from a wheelchair."

"Is a little more complicated with them. I can see this."

"You sort of start to wonder if you'll have anybody pure enough left to name anything after if you try to get rid of all these guys."

"We talked about this in one of my classes last year," I tell him, "around the time of Columbus Day. The teacher asked if those of us who are Hispanic should really be celebrating a man who was responsible for the genocide of so many in the countries that we came from. Moua said this would be like Cambodians celebrating Pol Pot Day."

"Columbus, though," he says, "didn't exactly start up all the atrocities in the New World. I'm pretty sure the Aztecs didn't pick up their human sacrifice rituals from him. Plus, you have to admit, whatever else you think of him, to cross the ocean in three little wooden ships like he did, with no real clue how big it was or what he would find on the other side, he had to have some serious *cojones*."

I smile at that. "I suggest you to learn Spanish, and *this* is the first word you show me?"

"Sorry. I know a few others, mostly stuff I picked up from guys in the Army. Nothing you would want to hear. You'll have to teach me some better ones."

"This I will be glad to do."

He tells me that his professor has encouraged him to try to write something about his experiences in the war, maybe even get it published. He has spoken before of writing a book about war, so I know this is something important for him to hear.

"I'm glad he's encouraging you," I say. "But I think I would rather read something you write about helping to raise your four little brothers."

He smiles. "A lot of people have done that, though. Not so many have been blown up in Afghanistan."

"I'm so glad you made it home."

"Me, too."

Then he asks me to be his girlfriend. He says he isn't going to put any pressure on me about anything else—and of course I know what he means by that—but he is ready to make a commitment to dating me exclusively if I am ready to make that commitment to him. I was ready to do that two weeks ago, but I don't tell him that. Tori will say I should have told him, "Give me some time to think about it," just to keep him squirming for a little while, let him know who is in control, but I don't want to play those games with him. I tell him I am ready.

No movie could have been as good as this. I'm *feliz como una lombriz* when he drops me off at home and gives me another kiss, the best one yet. He's a great kisser. Then I go in and find out what Morgan has done.

I had turned my phone off while I was with Eduardo, one of the rules we both sort of figured out to do for each other without even discussing it. Moua is the one who gives me the news about what happened at the house, and then I retrieve Clara's voice mail message and find out about the café. I run right to my room, and it makes me sick to my stomach as soon as I go in. I never had much stuff, but anything of value that I had, Morgan has taken, including a silver locket my mother gave me that has been in our family for more than a hundred years. I kick myself for leaving it in the room; I had almost put it on before Eduardo picked me up, but I didn't want to seem like a show-off. She will probably sell it for ten dollars when it is worth at least a thousand—and worth way more than that to me. She had grabbed what little cash I had on hand, of course, which I was planning to send to my family: what buys almost nothing here can still go a long way in Mexico. In that second I hate her, more than I did when I realized she had abandoned her baby. And then, with my heart in my throat, I realize I haven't even asked about Brianna.

Moua has come into my room right behind me. She reads my mind before I can ask.

"Brianna was in Martha's room with her and the g-ma. She's still here. I was in mine, so Morgan didn't get my stuff. She opened my door without knocking, and she looked a little weird, so that's why I checked on your room a little later. She hit Tori's, too, and pretty much cleaned her out. Tori is going to be pissed."

Tori is going to be ready for nuclear war.

I know she's going to blame me, and she'll be right, but in the moment I somehow don't care. I just want to see Brianna and hold her and know that Morgan did not take from this house the only part of it that truly matters.

CHAPTER 30

MOUA

So *cleaned out* turns out to be a bit of an exaggeration. Tori has a lot more stuff than the rest of us. Guys have been giving her tons of gifts to try to get into her pants probably ever since she hit puberty. I've seen a glamor shot of her when she was twelve, and she already looked like she was eighteen then. That room of hers was packed. There's no way Morgan could have carried off all of that. She went for the jewelry, of course, which was probably mostly costume crap and not really worth all that much, but I'm still expecting Tori to rip Alicia to pieces when she gets home. Maybe even take the rest of her stuff that Morgan missed and move out.

I'll admit I never liked Tori. It's not just because she's so perfect-looking or because she puts it in my face that I'm not. I just don't like her attitude in general. If she's not whining about her dates, she's complaining about her boss at the restaurant who calls her out when she's late, or her mother who calls to try to borrow money that Tori claims she barely has enough of to pay her own bills. That last is Tori in a nutshell: in one breath she's bragging about all these great tips she rakes in, like she's halfway to her first million, and in the next she's acting like she doesn't have a dime to her name to help out a family member. I admit, her mother is seriously messed up, but if Tori thinks she's got problems there, she should meet mine sometime. She's always complaining about school, too. If she would just study a few hours every day instead of depending on a last-minute cram session to get by every time, that would solve most of her problems with her GPA, which at this rate is not going to get her anywhere near the nursing program. Her boss would probably get off her back, too, if she just got to work on time once in a while. It doesn't really seem like too much for a boss to ask, does it?

Of course, I can't really relate to the tardiness issue because my own hours on the job are completely flexible—another one of the advantages of the phone sex biz. Which, I admit, Tori would totally kick ass at if she were sensible enough to give it a try instead of flaunting her flesh at the restaurant. How much better than being a prostitute is *that*, anyway?

When Tori gets home from her shift, Alicia goes straight to talk to her. That's just the way Alicia is. I'm wondering if I should take cover somewhere or cut off the necrophiliac I'm on the phone with in case I need to call 9-1-1.

I pretend to listen to my creepy caller as I crack my door open and watch, expecting the worst. I almost drop my phone when I see what happens. Tori just listens for a minute in the doorway and then puts her arms around Alicia and tells her not to worry about it, it's just stuff. Alicia starts to cry, of course, and Tori's just standing there in her uni with her Miss Universe mammary glands still on the job, patting her on the back and listening to her sob and trying to comfort her, like it's Alicia and not her who just got the terrible news. Then they go together into Alicia's room, where Alicia has the baby now after getting her handed off from Martha and the g-ma. The next thing I see, Tori comes out holding Brianna and making goo-goo eyes and rubbing noses with her, and I think either I must be hallucinating or I've been transported to a parallel universe where Tori actually gives a shit about someone besides herself.

I close my door and go back to my phone and get my grave robber off, then pick up the assignment for this stupid research paper I have to write for my history class, but I can't really concentrate on it. I keep going back to what I saw through the doorway instead. *Just when you think you know someone.*

CHAPTER 31

TORI

I been robbed before. It don't faze me. Nothin' nobody can steal from me is gonna take away who I am or what I'm gonna be in this life. The one I feel for is Alicia. She put her trust in that slut Morgan, went way out on a limb to help her, and damned if the sorry-ass skank didn't just saw it right off from under her.

Alicia got to learn: it's okay to help other people, but you always got to look out for your own self, too. Growin' up on the south side, you learn that shit real quick. Be all kinds of brothers and sisters down there doin' their thing to *help the community*, but they always lookin' to get some helpin' for theirself, too.

Just like that damn minister who tried to finger-fuck me when I was eleven. Mama didn't believe me, thought I was makin' that shit up. How could a man so respected in the community, a man who raised thousands of dollars to clothe and feed the poor, to shelter the homeless, a fuckin' *giant* of a man, how could he possibly do something like that to an innocent little girl? Then when Mama goes to talk to him, get some advice about how to handle her crazy-ass daughter, he pulls the same shit on her. She saw things a little different after that, but it was a little too late for me. That's when I learned the only person you can really count on in this life is yourself. If even your own damn Mama won't take you at your word or take your side when some fool tries to mess with you, who else you ever gonna be able to trust when you need help the most? All you really got is you.

I count up the shit I lost and put away my tips from today's shift, including a big fat one from Eduardo. Maybe Latin Batman tryin' to send me a subliminal message there, like he can make time for a fine-lookin' sister if Alicia hold out too long on givin' him some pussy. Then I remember I got a test tomorrow I ain't even started to study for yet. Moua got the same class. I go knock on her door. She on the phone, as usual, makin' some money, but she lets me in and goes into a corner to finish her business. I look around her room. It don't look like she lost nothin' to our little live-in thief. Asian people, you got to give them credit, they know how to hang onto their shit. Over in her corner, she gives up this really cheesy fake orgasm that wouldn't fool a first grader, then listens for a minute and hangs up.

I pass on the chance to give her some acting tips and get right to the point.

"You got some notes I could borrow for the chemistry test tomorrow? I been so busy at work, I ain't had time to study for it."

"You don't take notes for the chem class while you're waiting tables at The Roadkill, do you?"

She always got to give me some lip. Most times, I'd make her pay for that, show her how to talk trash for reals, but it's getting late, and I need to get the notes and get some sleep, so I let it go. The sleep I can maybe do without, but I really need those damn notes. Maybe I can even get her to coach me up a little bit if I don't bite her mouthy little head off first.

"How 'bout we go over those notes you got, together?"

"I've been busy at work, too," she says. She holds up her phone to remind me. "And I've got a research paper that's due tomorrow for my stupid history class."

"You done the research yet?"

"Not really. Enough to fake it and get an A."

Moua's all about the A's for her GPA. She a whiz at math and science, does good in all of her other classes, too, but she hates to write papers. I guess she use up what little bit of creative shit she got on the phone.

I took the same class last semester. I see a little window here.

"I wrote a paper for that class," I tell her. "Got an A on it, too. Unless Morgan scooped it up when she hit my room, I still got it in there somewhere. Different teacher, but a lot of 'em use the same assignments. Close enough to fake it, anyway, like you say. How 'bout I fetch it, and you could take a look at it, get some ideas from it, long as you don't copy too much, get us both in trouble? Save you some time gettin' started anyway. If you could share your chem stuff, I mean."

"What's the paper on?"

"Underground Railroad. Harriet Truman."

"Tubman."

"Whatever."

"I hope you spelled her name right in your paper."

"I got an A, didn't I?"

"I don't know, did you?"

"Let me go get it. Back in a flash. Get them chem notes ready."

It takes me a few minutes in the mess Morgan left, but I find the paper, go back and hand it over, wait to get the chem notes from her, which by now I'm almost too tired to even glance at. I wonder if there's a way I can keep them on my desk while the test is goin' on. Depends on what kind of mood Professor Little Old Man be in. Some test days he be all whacked out on caffeine, be stompin' up and down the aisles like the damn border patrol lookin' for wetbacks crossin' under your truck. Other days he just chill and sit up front readin' his newspaper while we dyin' over his braintwisters. You could take your top off in the front row, and he wouldn't even look up from his business section, checkin' his investments. He a real Heckle and Jeckle when it come to proctoring a test. Never know which one you gonna get till you get there. Guess it depend on how the stock market doin' that day. I figure I'll take the notes with me and give it a shot if he chillin'. I'm so tired now I know my eyes will close as soon as I look at one page.

Moua checks the last page of my paper and finds the A, just like I said. That's all she needs to see.

"This could work."

She hands over the notes.

"Don't use too much of that essay," I tell her again.

"Don't worry about it. I'll just take a quick glance to get some ideas, or maybe lift a few quotes. Besides, like you said, it's for a different teacher, and they read like a million essays every semester—or pretend to, anyway. What are the chances of anyone noticing two papers out of a million that might be a tad similar?"

I'm too tired to argue with her. She's probably right, anyway. Half of the time when you write a paper at the college and get it back, you can't even tell if the professor really even looked at it. Just go to the back like Moua just done and find the grade and maybe some little comment, like "Great job!" if it's an A or "Good work!" if it's a B. Same shit as high school. Easy-ass job, if you ask me. Too bad it don't pay worth shit.

Down the hall I hear Brianna wake up and start cryin'. Alicia up in a heartbeat to feed her and change her. Look like me and Moua ain't the only ones who'll be draggin' our sleepy asses around come morning.

CHAPTER 32

EDUARDO

We're finally making plans for that movie date we've been trying to get to since the second time we met. The movie Alicia originally suggested has left the theaters, and we can't find anything else playing now that either of us wants to see, so I suggest that we rent a DVD and watch it at her house or my apartment. I figure she'll pick her house for our first time to do this, but she doesn't have a TV, let alone a DVD or Blu-Ray player, in her room, and she says it's impossible to guarantee any privacy in the living room. Tori might bounce through the door at any moment and either hit on me or demand an audience to listen to her rag on the colossal loser she just dumped after one date. Martha might burst out of her room in a fever dream and try to form us into a prayer circle in the middle of a big sex scene—not that I'm planning on renting a movie with one of those, but you never know when a producer is going to try to put some butts in the seats by putting some skin on the screen. Alicia doesn't say much about what Moua might do, but I can tell she's got something going on that might not help to make our first movie night a success at Violet's house. Alicia agrees to come to my apartment instead. I promise to be on my best behavior.

"Well, in that case, maybe I won't bother to come."

She gives me a sly smile when she says this, and I realize that maybe she is ready to go faster than I thought. Our goodnight kiss as we seal the deal is the most promising one yet.

I practice for the Indianapolis 500 on the way home and then spend a good two hours scrubbing my apartment. Fortunately, the Army taught me how to keep things clean. I wasn't a complete slob before I went in, but my mom still loves to remind me that there's a big difference between *man-clean* and *woman-clean*. Alicia's going to be a doctor, so I know this stuff matters to her. I don't want her to walk into my place for the first time and choke on a dust bunny as she comes through the door.

We have a hard time deciding what movie to see, even on DVD, but eventually we sort of agree that it doesn't matter so much. We'll have fun as long as we're together. She leaves it up to me. I finally decide to pick up a film by a Mexican director that won an Oscar for Best Director. I know this will impress Alicia. Actually, Mexican directors have won four of these awards since 2014. Even though I'm not normally big on sci-fi and passed on this one when it was in the theaters, I've heard enough about how unusual it is to give it a chance now. We watch it in Spanish, of course, with English subtitles for me.

Alicia loves it.

She's gripped from start to finish and falls in love with the main character. I start to get a little jealous of the fish-man. She didn't fall in love with me anything like as fast as that. It reminds me a little of the first time seeing her with Brianna. At least for a couple of hours this movie is taking her mind off worrying about the baby and getting ripped off by Morgan. I just hope Martha doesn't get any goofy ideas about welcoming Morgan back to the fold if she tries to come crawling back with some pathetic excuse for what she did now.

I'm not quite as crazy about the movie as Alicia is, but at least it keeps me guessing. One thing I can't stand is a movie where you can predict everything that's going to happen way before it ever does. So many movies are like that, but this one isn't. I see some scenes that I haven't seen a thousand times before, and I never know for sure what's going to happen next, up until almost the very end.

Another thing I appreciate is that this movie passes the "Are you okay?" test. By which I mean that this stupid line of dialog is never said in this movie by one character to another after the second one has just been shot, stabbed, hacked with a sword, bludgeoned with a tire iron, or run over by a speeding vehicle. And/or after he or she has just watched from close range in horror as his/her comrade, partner, best friend, only child, or the love of his/her life has been beheaded by a rocket-propelled-grenade or dismembered by an angry bear. So many crap movies put the main character into this situation, inches from experiencing agonizing death, or witnessing it, and a minute later somebody's chirping "Are you okay?" into his/her ear while wiping the blood off his/her face and applying a Band-aid to a wound that would have dropped a buffalo. And then in the next scene, of course, the hero/heroine is perfectly fine, often without a scratch or the slightest sign of trauma showing. Even some otherwise pretty decent movies have been known to include a sequence like this. I think the Screen Writers Guild must have negotiated a clause in their contract that says "Are you okay?" (or its clever variation, "Are you all right?") has to be in 98% of all the movies that get made. Next time you watch a movie, give it the test. I bet you'll see what I mean.

Fortunately, we don't hear (or read) the line tonight. Alicia's smiling, wiping away tears, as the movie ends. I ask if she wants to take a look at the Special Features. Of course, I'm secretly hoping she'll say, "Let's skip those and hop into bed. You can show me *your* special features instead." But she's interested enough to say yes, and since I was stupid enough to ask, we watch those, too, and she's fascinated all over again with the details of what went into making the film.

Even though my priorities are elsewhere, I have to admit that these extras aren't bad. Sometimes they're so awful I want to eject the disk, throw it straight into the garbage disposal, and grind it into a million tiny pieces. So many times it's the whole main cast falling all over themselves to call this magical movie they've created the greatest thing put on film since Charlie Chaplin. They're sitting around in a circle-jerk telling each other how fabulous they all are and what a genius the director is and how the leading actor and actress are the only performers in the history of the cinema who could possibly have done justice to their roles. Some guy who tried to sing in the movie and sounded like he was gargling with carbolic acid is the next Sinatra. They don't talk about the writer as much or show his face, but he's clearly going to knock Shakespeare into second place. By the time you finish listening to this crapfest, you wish you'd never heard of the movie in the first place.

Just once I'd like to see a special feature where the actors say the director was a real pain-in-the ass to work with and couldn't keep his hands off the Best Boy. The leading man was drunk on the set every day, forgot half of his lines, and mumbled the rest like Marlon Brando with his mouth full of marbles. The leading lady was screwing the Assistant DP and threatening to sue if so much as a single close-up of her butt wound up getting cut. The writer shows up this time to say that not a single word of his original screenplay survived because the director just wanted to find three or four more scenes where he could squeeze in "Are you okay?" Now *that* would be a special feature worth spending an extra fifteen minutes on. That might actually feel halfway real.

I admit, though, I wind up getting more caught up in the extras that I'm watching now than I expected to. When we reach the end of the last one, I look over next to me and see that Alicia has nodded off. I remember how hard she has been working in school and at Clara's café, and how much taking care of Brianna is wearing her out. I just sit there looking at her beautiful face for a few minutes and letting her sleep. Then I wake her gently and take her home.

When we get there, we find out what has happened to Martha and Brianna.

Moua doesn't have all the details yet, but we listen in shock to what she does know. As she's running it down for us, I realize that Sergeant Mackey is back in the house he'd been banned from. He's trying to calm his ex, who is rocking and sobbing and praying like crazy in her wheelchair. Alicia starts to cry hysterically, too.

All I can think of is, if this were a movie, the line somebody would be saying to Martha right about now.

CHAPTER 33

OFFICER MASON

As soon as we reach the scene, I know I'll have to shoot the dog to save the girl. It's dusk, and I don't even see the baby on the ground at first and come damn close to hitting her, too. The pit bull's got the girl's arm in his mouth, so I can't risk aiming at his head as I run up. My first shot hits him squarely in the flank, but he still doesn't quit. He's shaking that girl's arm like he's for sure going to tear it right off. I don't get a good look at her face until after my second shot, into his skull from point-blank range, puts the dog down. He has mauled her pretty good. Then I see the baby. The dog has bitten clean through her abdomen, torn out a good chunk. I almost toss my cookies.

My partner has called for back-up, and two other cars get there quick to shoo off the neighbors who are swarming around and to get the girl and the baby into an ambulance and on the way to ER. I don't like that baby's chances of making it to tomorrow. I hope the girl isn't going to lose that arm. From what was left of her face, she's probably going to have to learn how to chew all over again. Lots of plastic surgery ahead of her, for sure.

After the ambulance leaves, I spot Santos crouching over the brute I shot. She's a dog fanatic, has two Labs at home, bigger than she is, that she yaps about all the time. I wouldn't be surprised if they sleep in her bedroom at night. God knows she doesn't let any men in there. She's actually petting the dead dog when I reach her side.

"I had no other choice," I tell her.

She nods. She's prickly but not crazy. "I wish you could have shot the owner instead. It's his fault this happened."

My turn to nod. "I'd rather have shot whoever owns him, too." *Owned*, I should have said.

I've had dogs myself my whole life, too, from the puppy I begged for as a little kid to the Shepherd I have now that used to ride with me on the job. I have zero patience with people who keep animals but don't understand that you have to treat them right. You spend the time it takes to discipline and train them properly, and you have the most loyal and reliable companion you could ever ask for—far more dependable than most people, who tend to take a powder the minute you really need them, kick you when you're down, or even stab you in the back. But if you neglect or mistreat a dog, fail to train him right, he can turn on you in the blink of an eye and mess up your life worse than any of those back-stabbers could ever dream of. Especially pit bulls. And with them, even the training might not be enough to overcome their instincts. I know their fans defend them and claim they can be made harmless, but I don't buy it.

One call I was on, down by the Crosstown Freeway, two of them went berserk and attacked the next door neighbor when he was just trying to feed them their regular meal while their owner was out of town. They chewed off half of his face and then went to work on his nuts. He never even made it to ER. Died from the trauma in the ambulance on the way. This is what he gets for being a Good Samaritan and helping out a neighbor. Talk about *No good deed goes unpunished.* I had to shoot both of those dogs, too. The owner replaced them within a month.

"Did you see the name on the tag?" Santos asks.

I bend over to read it, then just shake my head. "Somebody's idea of a joke. Is that even spelled right?"

"I'm surprised you'd notice. Did you even recognize that baby?"

I hadn't exactly been focusing on the baby's face, and, I'll admit it, other than my own kids, when it comes to babies I'm pretty much in the *seen one, seen 'em all* category. Santos is giving me that look of hers like I never should have made it through the Academy. Then it hits me:

"Is that the one we—"

"Yep."

"Oh, shit. Maybe we should've let that Mex waitress take her home after all."

"*Mex*?"

"Sorry. *Mexican*."

She's always busting my balls about stuff like that. I don't know why. She knows I don't have a prejudiced bone in my body. I'd fuck that good-lookin' brown-eyed gal just as long and strong as I'd fuck the Queen of Sweden.

She nods at my apology. "Maybe we should have. None of this would have happened then."

Half an hour later we've almost given up on him when the pit bull's owner shows up. We'd gotten his supposed-to-be work number, which turned out to be his cell, from a neighbor and told him to get here pronto or we'd come to his job and pick him up. He's a skinny dude, twenty-five to thirty, with his hair in dreadlocks and his pants sagging way down under his grundies. It's not too hard to figure out what kind of *work* he's been doing. He's holding up his pants with his left hand, and there's a cast on his right forearm. I catch myself speculating (okay, I admit it, *hoping*) that his own now dead dog tried to chew his arm off the last time he went to feed him or pet him. This assbag, though, looks like a better bet to punch his dog in the mouth than to pet him.

He's really pissed about losing the pit bull. He doesn't seem to give a shit about the girl the dog mauled or the baby it tried to eat. I hope someone will show him the photos from the scene, preferably a prosecuting attorney with a plan to put him away for a long time.

"You didn't have to kill him," he says. "How come you didn't just Tase him or something?"

My partner is right in his face. "How come you didn't keep him locked up like you're supposed to? How come you have an attack dog for a pet in the first place?"

"He never attacked nobody before."

Santos has already checked the computer records and learned that this isn't true. Several neighbors had filed complaints earlier about the dog menacing their kids on the way to or from school. She points this out. The guy doesn't seem to remember or care.

"Maybe someone was teasing him. Was you there? Did you see it?"

My partner groans and then swears under her breath. I think she'd pull her piece and put one in his peabrain right now if she could get away with it. I wouldn't mind if she did. I can tell you exactly how it would go down in the write-up, too: when he grabbed her gun from her, he dropped his pants, tripped over them, fell on his face as he was pulling the trigger, and accidentally shot himself right between the eyes.

"You never know how stupid people can be around dogs."

He has finally said something I can agree with.

My partner tells him to stay where he is while she makes a call. I know she's hoping to find out we can cuff him in front of the neighbors, who are still watching from their yards or their front windows. One of them comes out of her house while we're waiting to find out.

It's a fifty-something black woman with a *Don't fuck with me* look in her eye. She was the last one to leave the scene before at the other cops' urging, and she's the first one back. She heads right for him, and I have to step into her path to cut her off. She leans around me to shout at him.

"It's about time someone shot that fucking beast of yours. That's your own baby girl he just took a bite out of."

Santos and I look at each other and then back at her as if we can't trust what we just heard.

"Oh, yeah. I seen that baby girl here couple of times before, with her mama, not the one got ate up today. Her mama bring her around tryin' to find this fool. Better off lookin' for him down at the jail."

"Why don't you just mind your own business, bitch?"

If these two were to tangle, my money's on the *bitch*. She looks like she could take this clown down without working up a sweat. Of course it's my job not to let that happen, but I'll bet the whole neighborhood would celebrate if I just stepped out of the way and let her kick his over-exposed ass. He still looks more upset about what happened to his dog than about what happened to his daughter.

"Only reason my grandchildrens is in one piece is I keep watch out for 'em every single time they pass this fool's house," the neighbor says. "Damn dog been chasin' after 'em for years. I wish it had been me shot him." She turns back to our hero. "Like to shoot your stupid black ass, too."

Another precinct heard from. That makes it unanimous.

Unfortunately, word comes down from the station that we can't perform a summary execution. We can't even arrest the owner since he wasn't on the scene. It's possible that someone else opened up his gate and let the dog out—of course it should have been locked and impossible for the dog to get out—but the technicalities are in this guy's favor, at least until the case is investigated. I get right in his face and tell him we'll see him in court. My partner goes me one better.

"If that baby dies, I hope you get life in prison. Enjoy your stay in Pelican Bay."

CHAPTER 34

OFFICER SANTOS

We find out later it takes a team of surgeons working six straight hours to save the baby. She lost a kidney and a lot of blood, but they are finally able to stabilize her condition and keep her breathing, at least for now. She's not out of danger by any means, but at least she's alive. Mason wants to know what the hospital's bill for all of this will be, not that there's any chance it will ever be paid by the guilty party, just absorbed by taxpayers like us who carry deadbeats like him on our backs.

Another team of surgeons saves the other girl's arm and stitches up her face, although she may still lose sight in one eye where the dog bit near the optic nerve. It could have been a lot worse for her, that's for sure, if Mason hadn't done what he did.

My partner can be a pain-in-the-ass—*is* just that most of the time, in fact— but I have to admit when the shit comes down, he knows how to do his job. A lot of cops—including maybe me— would have been afraid to shoot, with the girl's arm still in the dog's mouth, but Mason didn't hesitate. Who knows, with one more violent side-to-side jerk, the dog might have torn that arm all the way off. It was close to being severed as it was.

Mason tells me later he saw the stroller but didn't realize it was empty. He didn't see the baby on the ground right next to the dog and the girl, or he might not have taken the first shot. I liked that he didn't bullshit me about that, pretend that he's infallible, like the public seems to expect us to be in those hairy situations. God knows if he'd missed the dog and killed the baby, he'd be the scapegoat of all time, just like those friends of his in our department who got reamed in the media for trying to save that bank hostage.

He told me that this makes six dogs that he's had to shoot on the job, half of them pit bulls. The interesting thing is that in eighteen years on the force, he's never had to shoot a human being. With all the kinds of duty he's drawn and all the gangbangers in this town, there had to be plenty of chances. He's been able to stick with his training and use other methods to defuse situations, even those where his own life or another cop's was threatened. As full of shit as he can be at times, you have to give him some serious credit for that.

We both jawed some at the scene about doing it, but I've never had to shoot anyone either, and I hope it stays that way. Sometimes I worry that I'll turn into some kind of a maniac like Duterte, the President who brags about murdering all the pimps and prostitutes and drug dealers and gangsters in Manila. When you see what a cop sees every day, even here, it's easy to start thinking that this is the answer, but of course we can't let ourselves turn into the same kind of monsters we are trying to keep under control. Mason told me once that he's really hoping to get his last two years in without having to kill anyone. He seems like the kind of guy who could handle it if he had to, but at least it's good that he's not looking to go out like a cowboy with his pistol blazing.

I thought a lot afterward about what I said right before we left the scene. Of course, we're not supposed to say stuff like that to civilians, but I just couldn't help myself. Now that it looks like the baby might survive, I wonder how that will play out. If she lives but can't lead anything resembling a normal life because of the injuries resulting from her own father's neglect, how does that factor into what a judge or jury decides about *him*? How do we hold one person accountable when his negligence destroys the health, if not the life, of another?

I love dogs more than anyone I know, but I have to admit that the people in this state are completely insane when it comes to regulating them. Our clueless legislature even passed a law that *forbids* the banning of private ownership of any species, including the violent ones. That makes about as much sense as the laws that prevent us from keeping AK-47s out of the hands of mental patients. Mason says we should keep a set of the photos from the scene with us in the squad car. If we hear one more idiot try to tell us that the killer instinct can be bred or trained out of pit bulls, we'll pull the pictures out, stick them in his face, and then stuff them down his throat. Mason will love leaving it out of his report.

I just hope he gets his twenty in without having to shoot anyone. I hope he doesn't have to shoot any more dogs either.

CHAPTER 35

TYREKE

motherfucker shot hittler i had that dog eight years thats my family lets see how that fatass like it when i fuck up *his* family fuck up that midget flip bitch he with too got a big mouth on her should of told her what she can do with it next time i see her i gonna show her instead

CHAPTER 36

MOUA

So Martha comes home today looking like something out of a made-in-the basement slasher flick. To start with, she's got bandages all over her face. She still might lose sight in one eye, and her right arm is immobilized in a cast and a sling. It's going to be hell for her on the hopper for a couple of months at least, that's for sure. I'll probably get drafted to help her, just like I help the g-ma, and what tons of fun that is. If the g-ma would just drop a hundred pounds or so, that would make it so much easier. As is, it's like lifting the rear end of a horse, or maybe a hippopotamus. Martha's no size zero herself, so it won't be any piece of cake positioning her to take a dump either. I just hope she doesn't expect me to wipe her afterward like the g-ma does. It's enough to make you seriously start to reconsider your major.

What happened was, a few days after she got baptized and before she robbed us and took off, Morgan was talking with Martha and told her about the guy who is probably Brianna's father. It's not like 100% certain: Morgan apparently hasn't been any more exclusive with her twat than I am with my phone, but she's pretty sure it's this guy who just got out of jail again and is back living in his mother's duplex, not that far from the g-ma's house. So Martha gets the bright idea that this might be where Morgan took off to and decides to go pay her a visit, with Brianna in tow. The plan was to put the baby in her face and see if she can get Morgan to come back to live with us. I guess the other part of the plan was to say we forgive her. It was just Martha and maybe the g-ma who came up with all this, because Alicia and Tori never want to see Morgan again, and neither do I.

Anyway, Martha takes Brianna out in her stroller, and it takes only a few minutes to walk to the duplex. That's the crazy thing about Stockton: we've got all of these zoning laws requiring builders to put up low-income housing wherever their developments go in, even the ritzy ones, so the neighborhoods are all mixed up, decent ones right next to the trashy ones. Martha and Bri are just a few blocks from home but on a street where the dealers hang out right in the open and cops are always being called to break up fights or track down gunshots.

So Martha finds the place where her baby-daddy is supposedly staying. The doorbell doesn't seem to work. There's a gate, which is unlocked, so she opens it to go knock on the door. Then suddenly this pit bull comes tearing out from the backyard and races right out through the gate into the street. It goes straight after some kids, who are out there playing in the street. Martha sees this and claps her hands and calls the dog and tries to get him to come to her, to get him away from the kids. She's probably planning to pet him and get like a great big slobbery kiss as a reward. The dog comes tearing back through the gate, knocks over the stroller, and instead of kissing Martha, takes a big bite out of Brianna. Martha screams and grabs him by the ears. He bites her face and then clamps his jaws around her arm and tries to tear it off. A neighbor sees it all right from the start and calls 9-1-1, or they'd both be history by now.

One thing about seeing what happened to Martha and Bri is it helps me to put my own problems into perspective. At least a pit bull didn't try to eat me. I'm trying to keep that in mind while I figure out how to handle what did go wrong for me.

What happened was that paper I copied from Tori for my history class wasn't such a risk-free venture after all. Turns out she copied most of it herself from a paper that's in the Turn-it-in. com file. She didn't say anything about that to me when I got it off her. I should've known better, of course. When did she ever stay home or sit still long enough to write a legit A paper?

Anyway, my stupid history teacher wrote this really pissy note on my paper when he handed it back. He said under the rules of the college's Academic Integrity Policy, he can flunk me, not only for the essay but also for the whole class, and he can even try to get me expelled. All this for one paper in a stupid G.E. class that doesn't even help with my major.

Tori acts like it's no big deal when I tell her about it. She doesn't even apologize for giving me a plagiarized paper to plagiarize from! I feel a little better when I find out she bombed the chem test, even with my notes, which she probably studied for all of five minutes, if that. She says my teacher probably just wants me to kiss his butt and say I'm sorry and I'll never do it again, and he'll let me do the paper over. Or if not, she says, I should slip the prof my business card, see if I can get him to give me a call, then blackmail my way out of this mess. It's actually not a bad idea. He looks like a guy who probably has to settle for phone sex anyway.

When Alicia comes home, I give her the latest update from the hospital about Brianna: now there's an infection that's threatening her life. Alicia cries, of course, and I wonder, *how much bad luck can one baby have?*

Your guess is as good as mine when Martha's going to be able to look in the mirror and figure out a way to explain how all this is part of the G-man's plan for her life. While she's praying on that, maybe she can get Him to tell her about His plan for Brianna's life, too.

CHAPTER 37

MARTHA

Heavenly Father,

Please forgive me for missing church the last few weeks. I'm sure You know, since You know everything, that I got hurt, in fact, I almost got killed. I've been busy trying to recover. I'm sorry that I have been missing my prayers lately too, usually I try to talk to Pastor Greg or Grandma Vi about my problems, but Pastor Greg says he's too busy to help me right now, and Grandma Vi can't really talk anymore, or at least I can't make out what she's trying to say. Can You? Of course You can, stupid question, I'm sorry.

I want you to know I don't blame anyone for what happened to Bri and I, I don't even blame the dog, he was just doing what he was trained to do, or what he was not trained not to do, I don't know which is a better way to say it. I forgive whoever left the gate unlocked, too, they probably just forgot. I hope You can forgive me for whatever I did that made You decide to punish me in this way, if it was for the baby I didn't have, I'm so sorry. I'm grateful that my arm didn't come off, I hope You will help my eye to get better. I know that many others, including Grandma Vi, have it much worse than I do. I know it's all part of Your plan, I guess You are testing all of us, like you did to Abraham and Moses and Job, to see if we can keep our faith when things go wrong. That's what Grandma Vi used to say when she could still talk, I guess You are the only One she can talk to now.

Tori says Moua got into some kind of trouble at school, I don't know what that is all about. I hope You can forgive her, too. She's always nice to me and tries to help me with my homework when she can. Sometimes she's too busy making phone calls, of course, but I understand. She's really smart, she even knows about the stock market, I guess she has made lots of money using her phone. I wish I was smart like her, maybe she can teach me how to make money with my phone like she does.

Even though I decided to write all this down, but I don't really know how to address it. I just wish I could send You a text or find You on Facebook. If there's any way You could let me know You got my message, I would really appreciate it, please forgive me if You can.

Your Faithful Servant,

Martha Shriver

P.S. Thank you for saving Briana's life after the dog bite, please don't let her die from the infection. After she gets better, please let Alicia bring her back to our house so we can take care of her here.

P.P.S. I didn't just get behind in church, I also got way behind in school. Please, please, please let me pass my math class this time, if I have to take that class again, I just might go back on the drugs You got me off before!

CHAPTER 38

NATALIE

This case has now become unquestionably the most unusual of my career.

When I was notified of the life-threatening injuries Brianna Hunt sustained, I was of course appalled and also angry at Martha Shriver for endangering her in that way. Martha herself has suffered potentially life-altering injuries that will inhibit her abilities to provide care for an infant, certainly for the short term and possibly for the long term as well. Compounding that circumstance, Violet Mackey suffered another stroke after she was informed of the attack upon her granddaughter and the baby. She was in no condition before, and certainly is in no condition now, to be the primary caretaker for the child. A prior stroke had resulted in her confinement to a wheelchair, and this second one further impaired her mobility and has also impaired her ability to speak. She will be needing twenty-four care herself now. An issue of uncertain origin has resulted in the displacement of one of the lodgers, Moua Sok, leaving only Alicia Gonzales and Tori Maxwell as able-bodied residents of the house. Both of them are working full-time or nearly full-time and going to school full-time, so to leave Brianna in their care would not be feasible even if she were healthy, which of course in the wake of her injuries and pre-existing conditions she is not. I am left with no choice but to recommend the active pursuit of other placement options for her. Finding someone who can provide the care she needs is going to be as daunting a challenge for the adoption agency as any I can imagine.

I decide to go to the house to try to deliver the news to Alicia personally, taking a chance that I will catch her there after school and before her restaurant shift. I am surprised to be met at the door by Jack Mackey.

I'm looking at him as if I don't understand what he is doing under his ex-wife's roof again after his well-chronicled banishment to the garage. He reads my confusion and cracks a small, wry smile.

"Moved back in when the gook moved out. Just in time, too: they locked up the restroom at the park across the street. Goddam homeless washin' their clothes in the toilet, then takin' an Olympic dump and can't be bothered to flush. There's piss and shit all over the floor."

I wince a bit at his description, although I know it's true and becoming epidemic, even on our streets. On the way over here today I passed a strip mall fronted by a row of stolen shopping carts loaded with all that some can call their own. In the middle of the sidewalk behind them a middle-aged white man was stooping with his pants down around his ankles to do his business for all the world to see. I don't point it out now, but if not for his ex-wife's forbearance, Jack would be homeless himself.

"I'm glad you have a better place to stay."

He shrugs. "Somebody got to take care of the old lady."

"How is she feeling?" comes out automatically.

"How would *you* be feeling if you were stuck in a damn chair all day, can't take a piss or a shit without help from your crazy ex-husband that you kicked out of the house before because you hate his guts, and you can't even complain about it now because your words don't come out clear no more?"

It strikes me that I may have just been on the receiving end of a new world's record in the category of rhetorical questions.

"It's good of you to help her," I say, not knowing where else to go with this.

He decides for me. "Nobody here to take care of that crack baby, though, so I hope you ain't here to tell us you're bringin' it back."

I wince again, at the *it*, and then shake my head. "I just came to let Alicia know that it won't be possible for her—or rather for Violet—to adopt Brianna."

"Alice ain't here. Went with Martha on the bus to the hospital to get some therapy that won't do shit. I'll give her the message, though."

"Thank you. Please tell her to give me a call."

I start to go when I hear, "You see what that pit bull did to Martha and that baby?"

"I've seen the photos."

"I suppose you don't favor capital punishment for the owner?"

"I don't favor capital punishment under any circumstances."

He nods. "Figures. What's your solution then? A fine? A spanking? You probably don't even believe in that. You part of the Dr. Spock fan club?"

"To some degree. I don't agree with corporal punishment either."

"I'll tell you what: if the fucker that owned that dog had got his ass kicked a few thousand times when he was a little shit, maybe he would have learned his lesson by now—and my granddaughter would still have a face."

I think of asking him if he found physical punishments helpful in raising his own children, and if the outcomes of their lives reassured him that his methods were sound. This borders on cruelty, though, since I'm aware of their fates, so I keep the sophistry to myself and walk back to my car. Considering the carnage he has just referred to, there is no use trying to end *this* conversation on an upbeat.

I go home and write my final report. Alicia calls later to ask if there's any hope for an appeal, and I have to tell her no, at least for the time being. In the silence that follows I can hear her heart break.

As I set down the phone and reach to pour myself another glass of wine, I suddenly find myself sobbing. I even spill a bit of the wine. I wonder if I have finally hit that infamous burnout point that everyone I have ever met has seen fit to tell me about. It might be time to heed the counsel Dad was always trying to give me, to find a less stressful and more satisfying occupation. Maybe it's time to go back to finish that credential I started on years ago and try my hand at teaching.

CHAPTER 39

BOOKER

If there were one thing that *could* make me consider retirement, it would be more faculty meetings like the tire-fire I just sat through. I'd rather sit for waterboarding by the CIA than any more sessions like that. It's not enough that we have the state legislature tying our funding to *Student Success* and our administration practically ordering us to give out grades like Halloween candy; now we also have to listen to junior faculty casually dismantling a curriculum some of us spent a lifetime building, and lecturing us on the fallacy of our *deficit-based* teaching methods. Some of them haven't even learned to speak or punctuate properly. How they ever made it through high school, let alone graduate school, is a mystery to me. I just heard one of them use *Me* as the subject of a sentence, another use *I* as the object of a preposition, and a third somehow manage the combination *her and I*. That's not just how they talk, either. They bombard the campus with email propaganda in which they ramble incoherently and forget (if they ever learned in the first place) to use a mid-sentence semicolon when attempting to scale the rhetorical heights of *however*. No wonder our students speak and write that way.

Deficit-based. What does this mean except pointing out the mistakes that students make so that they have at least a chance to avoid repeating them? How can they avoid them in the future if they don't know what they are? If a basketball player can't shoot free throws, he shoots a hundred—or a thousand—after every practice if he expects to earn any playing time in the games. I promise you would never hear Coach Pendleton—or any other coach—at practice saying, *Don't worry about missing your free throws. It probably won't cost us the next game. We'll probably lose anyway.* If students don't have a basic understanding of history, if they can't write sentences or paragraphs that make sense, if they can't construct an argument that reflects an understanding of what they were supposed to read, they have to be shown the error of their ways and to be held accountable for improving. Students need to be challenged, confronted with their weaknesses, instructed and pushed hard to get better, not encouraged to carry forward the shortcomings of their high school learning or to rely upon special consideration for their race or disability or sexual orientation. Don't try to tell a black man who earned a PhD in the 1970s that the discrimination today's students face prevents them from achieving their academic and career goals.

The teachers students remember and appreciate, even revere, are not those who pat them on the back and extend their deadlines and pass out easy A's, but those who require them to get their work done on time and inspire them to bring out their best, those who prepare them for the competition they will face after the picnic of academia has run its course. I still get letters and emails every semester from students—of all colors and preferences—who took my class in the past, some of them many years ago, thanking me for *not* letting them take the primrose path, telling me how the standards I set and pushed them to reach helped them to get into Berkeley or Davis or UCLA and to achieve their career goals in spite of the many obstacles that they faced. A surprising percentage of these are from women, who have remembered and appreciated, often in regretful hindsight, the two pillars of advice I routinely offer them in my rare departure from course-related instruction:

1. Don't marry an asshole.

2. Even after you have ignored #1, don't have children until you have put yourself in a position to support yourself—and them—by finishing your education.

I hear back from a few of the men, too, including some of those *kids*, now well into their fifties, whom I tutored for Coach Pendleton. I try to be a role model for the African American males I meet now as well, although far too many of them drop my class when they find out how much work they have to do to pass it. Even some who didn't finish my class have let me know that they appreciated the message I boiled down to a single sentence for them:

Forget the 'fashion statement': turn your cap around and pull up your pants.

I'm tempted to fling a collection of these tributes to my guidance into the faces of those so sure of my obsolescence, but of course they are too busy proclaiming the superiority of their own *amazing* and *incredible* methods to pay any attention to the accomplishments of their elders, focusing instead only on our failures. I have to admit, these neophytes remind me more than a little of myself at that stage of my career, when I started out at CSU: so sure of the truths they are determined to speak to power, so unwilling to consider any more experienced point-of-view. If I had been willing to play the part of house slave then, if I had learned a few years earlier to keep my mouth shut at faculty meetings, to kiss the right administrative asses, and to serve on a few hundred useless committees, I might still be ensconced at Hayward State, instead of relegated to a junior college, which some folks around here now seem determined to turn into a junior high school. I won't be alive to see it, but I'll bet in twenty years another generation of educators will be just as contemptuous of the current crop's failures.

Meanwhile, here we sit in a city of three hundred thousand, without a legitimate state university campus of its own—while CSU sits on a billion and half dollar surplus instead of building one. More students who live here drive to Sacramento or Turlock (*Turdluck*, as one of my former students, condemned to commute there, redubbed that jewel of the valley and Mecca of international scholarship) than attend in their own home town.

Who can blame them when they see what passes for facilities at the pissant branch campus here? Some developer threw a bone to the city and knocked up a cardboard campus without even a decent library. In exchange he received rights to transform more of the richest farmland west of the Fertile Crescent into cookie-cutter half-a-million dollar mini-mansions on postage stamp tracts, for the fakers who can't make it in the Bay Area, where the same houses cost three million. People like me, I guess you could say.

My wife has to have five bedrooms and three baths so our son and our daughters and their families can come home from New York and Chicago and Montreal to visit whenever the spirit strikes them. This, of course, is pure fantasy on her part. The reality is she's lucky if they remember to call on Christmas and send a card on Mother's Day or her birthday. Their batting average on Father's Day or my birthday is even lower, not that I need any more reminders of the years flying by. We hardly ever hear from them otherwise—except, of course, for the endless stream of solicitations for our grandchildren's iPads and Taekwondo lessons, and, of course, the sacrosanct annual pilgrimages to Orlando. Our kids couldn't wait to get out of the Central Valley, and they have very little desire to return, even for a holiday. I can't blame them too much. After all, I seldom went back to the land of cotton after making my own escape.

When I get home, my wife will be waiting for me to ask about her day. Maybe she will even turn down one of her televisions to encourage my conversation. Then I will get an extended replay of the latest inconceivably demented utterance or firing or hiring at the White House, or all three. And when her report is complete, she will want to know why I don't have more to say about my own day. But what can I say that I haven't said to her a thousand times before, that she wasn't interested in hearing then and won't be interested in hearing now, any more than I want to hear again about the insanity in Washington D.C.?

Maybe, for want of more inspiring matter, I will be reduced

to telling her tonight about the essay submitted by Ms. Moua Sok. It was easy to spot the plagiarism: how stupid do these students think we are? The young woman isn't stupid herself: I investigated her academic history, and she's thriving in a rigorous pre-nursing curriculum. She's just too bored or lazy to do her own research and writing, and too confident in the outcome of submitting someone else's essay. Obviously, there is very little fear of consequences. It will be necessary to remind her that some teachers on this campus still care about making students do their own work.

I have some latitude here. While some of my colleagues would just shrug this off, say "everyone makes mistakes" or chalk it up to "cultural differences" and allow her to write the essay again, a few of us are still prosecuting plagiarism cases vigorously. One philosophy professor hereabouts in particular is adamant about this. He's an Ethics man, somehow simultaneously steadfast in his support for the founder of Trump University, who prosecutes every case of academic dishonesty that crosses his desk. Rumor has it that he favors amputation at the elbow for the first offense and the firing squad for the second. I'm not entirely out of sympathy with him, especially when the students insult our intelligence by attempting to deny their malfeasance. We'll see what our Ms. Sok has to say for herself when confronted with the evidence.

I will have to be careful here. A student who would cheat so blatantly on an essay is capable of other forms of treachery. One student's accusation of impropriety, even if completely unfounded, can undo the course of a professor's career. Even one as inglorious as my own has turned out to be is worth protecting and preserving—especially when the alternative is retirement to TV Land.

CHAPTER 40

MOUA

So what happens at school could have been worse. When I get to Professor Bisson's office, I close the door behind me, thinking this is going to be super private, but the first thing he does is he makes me open the door back up, all the way. I guess he doesn't take any chances with being alone in there with a female student. It's probably a head-up policy. Even if the phone blackmail scam that Tori came up doesn't pan out, I could still make up some story about what he tried to do to me in his office. Maybe borrow some details from Morgan or from my callers since I don't have any actual experience in that department, and see if that will back him off on the cheating charges. The truth is I could probably ruin his reputation, mess up his whole life, just by making up some stuff like that. The real thing happens often enough, it's on the Internet and the TV news just about every day, so most people would probably just figure it was true and he'd get fired or at least suspended. I'm really tempted to give it a try, to pay him back for all the trouble he's causing me over one stupid paper that I copied part of—well, okay, all of—but I decide to listen to what he has to say first.

I look around as I sit down. On his desk he has pictures, obviously of his family. I check out one, and at first I think that must be him with his mother, but then I see another one with kids and grandkids, so I know it has to be his wife. She looks like she hasn't missed too many meals. She's twice his size, and he's no beanpole. I wonder when the last time they went to bed together was, and if they have even done this in the time that I have been alive; or if somehow they're active now, what safety precautions have to be taken when six hundred pounds of human flesh attempt to commingle. Do they need the Jaws of Life to be standing by? When I look at her, *big as a house* pops into my head; I can't help it. All of them in the photos look very well-fed, especially by comparison with the starving-in-the-death-camp look you'd see in any group photo of my family, if we ever took one. They all have perfect teeth, too, of course. I picture his whole inseparable clan getting together every Sunday for family dinner, praising the Lord for His bounty while happily tearing into platters piled high with pork chops.

He also has lots of photos on his walls. For a contemporary history prof, he has all the usual suspects—Martin Luther King, Cesar Chavez, Robert Kennedy—but I notice that he has a lot of women up there, too. He sees me looking and points at one of the photos.

"There's someone you should recognize."

I don't, but without even asking I know it's got to be the subject of my/Tori's essay. Harriet Tubman looks a bit like his wife, only much skinnier. I'm not sure if this observation would please him, so I keep it to myself. I just nod.

He points to the next picture. I draw a blank again.

"That's Rosa Parks," he tells me.

Now I remember. "The woman who wouldn't give up her seat on the bus. She started the Civil Rights Movement."

He looks at me like I'm three years old and just stuck a pencil in my ear to see if it would come out the other side. He sighs and then sort of smiles. "She didn't exactly start it, but she gave it a good hard push forward. It took a lot of guts to do what she did. Most of us will go through our lives without ever being in a situation to find out if we have that kind of courage or gumption."

I nod again. The only courage I've had to show so far was to get out of my mom's house. I also had the gumption to start my own business, of course, but I don't think that's anything I can share here, at least not yet. Although now that I've seen what his wife looks like, I don't rule it out completely.

Next to Rosa, I do recognize Dolores Huerta. There's a plaza named after her on our campus, and she even came to our high school one time to talk about her role in the Chicano movement. She told us that she was actually the one who did a lot of the work that Chavez got credit for. I mention this, figuring it can't hurt my cause.

He tells me that Dolores was a student at this college herself, in its previous incarnation on another campus. He's so old, I wonder if she was a student in his class. Of course, she's no spring chicken either, so I don't ask.

He also has that famous picture, which is in our textbook, of the naked Vietnamese girl running in the road and screaming while the napalm bombs go off behind her. There's one other Asian woman I don't recognize on his wall. At first it looks to me like she is another Vietnamese, but he tells me she's from Myanmar, which used to be called Burma. I know it's not too far from the part of Cambodia where my mom was born and stuck in that chicken coop.

"Her name is Aung San Suu Kyi," he says. I have to look it up later to get the spelling right.

"I think I've heard of her before," I lie, just to try to impress him.

"And what have you heard?"

So much for that idea. "I don't really remember too much."

"She led the freedom movement in her country. On one occasion she marched right into a line of raised machine guns pointed at her face and persuaded the regime's soldiers to put them down."

I look at her picture again. She looks more like an international film star than a revolutionary. I say something about how come a woman can lead a Third World country but we can't elect a woman President here. He reminds me that it doesn't help when almost half of the women in this country vote for a man accused by multiple sources of harassment or rape, a man who brags about grabbing women by their genitalia (unlike our President and many of my callers, the professor doesn't use the p-word). Then he tells me that this Aung San Suu Kyi won the Nobel Peace Prize, but now she's under attack from other nations around the world for failing to prevent her own country's massacre of the Rohingya Muslims, who are this generation's Boat People. I've never heard of them either, but I guess what's happening to her and them now goes to show that even the superheroes, who win the highest honors we hand out, have flaws of their own: nobody's perfect. Which seems like as good a lead-in as I'm going to get to make my case for a do-over on that essay I borrowed.

"I haven't had a B since the first grade," I tell him, "and that one was when I was out sick and the teacher forgot. Everything else since then is A's. An F is really going to mess up my transcript. Do you know how hard it is to get into the nursing program here?"

"Perhaps you should have taken that into consideration before you submitted somebody else's work."

I think for a second about throwing Tori under the bus here, see if I can cop a plea bargain and get a reduced sentence for myself, but he doesn't seem too interested in finding out where the essay I copied came from. He's definitely not interested in protecting my GPA. I even think about telling him about what happened to Brianna and how Alicia's still hoping to get custody of her and how much I'm helping, but I don't get the feeling that he's willing to consider any extenuating circumstances, no matter how much I dress them up.

The key to the whole deal is getting him to agree not to try to get me kicked out of the college if I admit what I did. I was hoping he would let me write the paper again and get rid of the F, but he says he's going to fail me for the essay and the course, so I will understand the consequences of what I did. He also says he's going to put a note in my file, and if I ever try anything like this again, I *will* get kicked out of school.

So the upshot is I have to take the stupid class all over again, but I can substitute the new grade after I repeat it and get rid of the F that way. As I'm hearing this, I'm thinking this time I'll do some research on ratemyprofessors.com and find a teacher who gives out lots of A's and doesn't throw a fit if you bend the rules a little bit. There's more of those kinds of teachers out there than you might think. The woman Tori took for the class is one possibility: she gets like a 95% 5 out of 5 rating from her students. One of the reviews, which I should have checked out before I took this dictator instead, says this:

Total kick-back class. This teacher literally does nothing except turn on the projector and then go for coffee. As long as you make sure to tack on a References page to whatever half-baked bullshit you copy and paste from the Internet into your research paper, that's all she checks—and the reader does that part for her. Trust me, I'm not exaggerating when I say if you just show up for class and kiss her ass, you're guaranteed to get an A.

Then I realize Professor Bisson is still talking. He's way ahead of me, and there's a kicker to his deal.

"I don't want you taking the easy way out of this. If you want me to agree not to press for your expulsion now, then when you repeat the class, you have to agree to take it again from me. Write your own research essay this time. Maybe you can learn a little more about one of the women on this wall. Those are my terms for this arrangement. Take it or leave it."

I don't even bother to give him my 900 number as I slink out the door.

CHAPTER 41

CLARA

Business been pretty good lately. Almost enough to make up for Morgan stealin' my cash. I know Alicia in a hurry to get out of here and meet up with her Romeo, but before she go, I'm gonna tell her she gettin' that raise she got comin'. Got somethin' else to tell her, too.

It ain't easy payin' out any more than minimum on what I clear here, but Alicia been workin' her tail off for me, and I know she need the money. Her school keep raisin' the fees on her every year, and them books she got to buy ain't exactly cheap neither. She told me one of 'em cost near two hundred dollars— second hand, you believe that? Got to be somebody out there makin' all kinds of money off all them poor students like her. Plus I know she still helpin' her folks down in Mexico as much as she can. Wish to sweet Jesus my own daughters was helpin' me from time to time by now, instead of still got their hands out for anything they can scratch off me.

She got more expenses comin' if she ever get to keep that baby she still after, 'specially now that it been chewed up by Man's Best Friend. As if that poor baby's life wasn't hard enough already, bein' borned to a thief and her jailbird boyfriend. Alicia got her work cut out for her there, just gettin' that baby back, let alone takin' care of her with all the problems she gonna have. Got to admire the girl though: she don't give up easy on what she believe in.

I see her clear the last table and gettin' ready to go home, get ready for the big date she got. Same time I see Miles from the

Food Bank comin' through my door with a smile for me almost as wide as he is. I hand Alicia a envelope with a little extra cash.

"This back pay for your raise, honey. You been doin' real good. You have fun tonight. I'm fixin' to have some, too. Before you go, someone here I'd like you to meet."

CHAPTER 42

TORI

Alicia look like she been cryin' again when I poke my head into her room. I figure she still fussin' about Brianna. I sit down on her bed and try to take her mind off her troubles by tellin' her mine.

"These fools I'm meetin' at school startin' to make Handsy Andy at work look a little more Toriworthy."

"What happened now?"

"Night start out okay. He take me to Red Lobster, tell me to order anything I want. I double-check and make sure we ain't splittin' this bill, then go for the Four-Course Feast. Halfway through the salad he start talkin' 'bout this old movie he seen on TV last night. I'm noddin' and eatin' and pretendin' to pay attention, and when the main course get there, I figure he'll shut up and hit that. But just keeps talkin', tellin' me every little detail of the plot, doin' the dialog, gettin' into the characters' voices, pretendin' he damn Robert DeNiro about to bash somebody's head in at the dinner table, the whole bit. Motormouth still runnin' when the dessert come. Now he 'bout to tell me the end of the damn movie."

If there's one thing I hate, it's people tellin' me the end of a book or a movie I'm plannin' to get to. All right, I admit, mostly movies since I don't get through that many books, what with work and school and goin' out with fools like this. He talkin' with his mouth full of chocolate mousse now, eyeballin' mine like maybe he gonna finish it for me if I leave a bite, fat fuckin' chance of that. I swear, a girl could say to this numbnuts, "Just shut the fuck up and drop your drawers, and let's take care of business right here, right now"—and he'd still keep right on talkin'.

"It's just a movie," Alicia says. She don't look like she really been listenin'. "Is it really that important if someone tells you the ending?"

"You damned right it is. I didn't sit there for two hours to have you spoil the climax for me. The only thing worse than that is when the damn movie doesn't *have* an ending. I hate that shit, too. You know, when the fools that made the movie can't make up their mind how to end it, or maybe they think it would be real clever for them to leave it up to you to decide? Like in *Three Billboards*, when the mother of the girl who got raped and murdered and the crazy racist ex-deputy she set fire to go off together to kill the guy who probably wasn't the rapist anyway, but we never find out if—"

"I haven't seen that movie yet. Maybe we could finish talking about it later."

It ain't like her to interrupt me, or anyone really, so I know now somethin' really bothering her. Time for *me* to shut up and find out.

"What up with baby girl?"

"Nothing," she says, and then she start to cry again.

That's when she tells me what a horrible thing Eduardo did to her tonight. You will not *believe* this shit.

CHAPTER 43

ALICIA

Tonight Eduardo and I had our first fight.

I had made plans to take him out to celebrate his birthday. I didn't tell Clara this part, but we went to Don Luis', a family-owned restaurant that is *his* family's favorite place to eat. As soon as we walk through the door—even before, actually, as we are waiting to get in—I can see and hear why. There is a loud mariachi band, and the whole place just *jumps* with energy and life. The room is absolutely packed, so I know the food must be good. Eduardo knows everyone working there by name, and they all know him and greet him as if he is a member of *this* family. When the menus come, I see that the prices are about halfway between Clara's and The Roadhouse's. The extra money Clara gave me will come in handy.

He is relaxed and happy in here. He asks me how school is going. I tell him that the time I spent with Brianna and trying to get her back got me way behind, but I have been working very hard to catch up. I ask him the same question, and he tells me that he has another paper back with more good news from Professor Bisson. When he says the name again, I remember that this is the same one who is going to flunk Moua and ruin her 4.0. Eduardo doesn't seem too surprised.

"He's definitely old school. You have to do your work if you want to pass his class. He's not going to give you a free ride just because you're a minority like he is."

"I guess she got what she deserves," I say. I still haven't told him how Moua earns her money. I'm not quite sure how he would handle that news. I ask him if he has made any more progress in deciding whether to focus on nursing or history.

"Or botany, don't forget," he says, with a laugh.

"Or business," I remind him, "which your father prefers. Maybe you can be the first student to complete a quadruple major in those four."

Another laugh. "It's crazy. In high school I wasn't interested in any of my classes. Now I'm interested in all of them. Sometimes I think what I'd really like to do is make movies."

He tells me about an Iranian movie that he saw in his film class. "It was just so real. There was nothing fake in it, like in so many movies. One of the characters, the grandfather, had Alzheimer's, which you almost never see in the movies made here, unless they make some stupid bathroom joke about an old man or woman who has gone senile, as if this is funny. This film was not like that. The way the family cared for the grandfather reminded me of what happened when my aunt got that disease, when I was just a little kid. When my uncle and my cousins finally realized they could not keep her at home, they had to put her in a care home. She was in a bed there for years, basically a vegetable, unable to speak or feed herself or use the toilet. My uncle went to visit her there every single day until she died. The movie was just as real, just as heartbreaking—to show in two hours what he and his family went through for almost twenty years."

"Maybe people have enough heartbreak in their lives," I say. "Maybe they go to a movie to get away from that, to be entertained instead."

"I think it is possible to do both at the same time. Of course, you have to find the right balance between having something to say and boring the shit out of the audience when you say it. I'm not saying it's easy, and certainly most movies fail at one or the other, or both, but I think it is possible when you get it right. I would love to try."

I can see the spark in his eyes as he speaks of this. He is not finished yet, either.

"Another thing I would love is to make movies that have lots people in them who look like you and me. You could go to a hundred movies made in the U.S. and never see a Latino character, or maybe there's one part for Michael Peña and nobody else, or a few crowd shots with token minorities in the background. Or if the Hollywood studios do make a movie about a real-life Latino hero, they cast Ben Affleck to play him. I would love to make movies that focus on people like my grandfather and my father, with actors who look like them."

I smile. "I thought you were going to write a book about them."

"I want to do that, too!"

"It seems you have almost as many careers in mind as Tori has boyfriends."

He laughs again.

"Will your movie be about what they did in their wars?"

"That would be worth making a movie about, for sure, but I think I'd be even more interested in showing what they did when they came back. There are so many clichés about veterans, so many stories in the media about the ones who went nuts and killed somebody later, but most of us just come home and do our best to fit back in, PTSD or not, and lead normal, productive lives—and most of us find a way to do it."

"Like your grandfather and your father have done with the nursery," I say.

He nods. "Of course, it will probably be pretty hard to sell a screenplay that takes place at a nursery: just watch those plants grow!" He smiles at his own small joke. "Oh, well. It's just a fantasy. I'll probably never get a chance to do anything like that."

"I think you can do anything you want to do. You can make your dream come true if you don't give up."

"Spoken like a woman who plans to be a doctor. Thank you for believing in me. I believe in your dream, too."

Things are going so well that I decide to take a big chance. At dinner probably isn't the right time to talk about this, but it has been on my mind so much that I can't help myself. I tell him that I still want to try to adopt Brianna even with all the medical issues she will be facing, and even if it takes a couple of years. I am prepared for him to tell me it is time to give up on that idea, like Ms. Robinson told me. Instead, he tells me that he admires me for sticking to my plan in spite of everything that has happened to Brianna.

"She will need help more than ever now. That is not the time to turn away from someone. And just because something is hard, that doesn't mean it isn't worth doing."

I reach out across the table and squeeze his hand. I know how hard he had to push himself to achieve his goal of becoming a Ranger, and how hard the fighting he had to do in the war was. He doesn't talk about that now, though. He talks instead about things he has been thinking of since he got out of the Army.

"When I was deployed, everywhere I went, all I could think about was how awful everything was for the people living there, and how much better we have it here. Maybe it would have been different if I'd been sent to Germany or Japan, and I'm sure a few fatcats in the Middle East have all the luxuries they want, but for most people there, life is just so primitive you can hardly believe it: the garbage in the streets, the open sewers, the smell you never get away from, the flies the size of bumblebees buzzing around you everywhere—these people live like this every day. I couldn't wait to get home."

I smile and squeeze his hand again. I think again how glad I am that he made it home.

"But now that I've been back for a while, I'm realizing that we need to pay more attention to the stuff that's not so great here. The other day I drove past the middle school I used to go to, and there were piles of litter all over the sidewalk and the playing fields. It looked more like a junkyard than a schoolyard. It really got me thinking about what a mess we have on our hands, right here in *the richest country in the world*. We send soldiers like me all over the world to fight everyone else's wars, but we don't clean up the trash in our own neighborhoods. Our roads are full of potholes—you can't go around the block without hitting at least one that's deep enough to screw up your alignment—and our schools are a disgrace. Half the time parents are afraid to even let their kids go to public schools now. We don't take care of the children in our own communities. We just let them become criminals and join gangs and try to take care of themselves."

"Like Brianna's father," I say.

He nods. "Exactly like him. Who wants a future controlled by guys like that? If we don't look out for our neighbors, for our own community, for the babies and the children who will grow up here, who else is going to do it for us? Those kids are the ones who will decide what life will be like for the rest of us when we are older. If we don't take care of them now, why should we expect them to take care of us later? We should tackle the problems that are right in front of us before we try to solve the world's. If we can help Brianna, that's a step in the right direction."

I am so happy to hear him say this, of course, and even happier when he says a moment later that he'd like to help me get my parents to the U.S. legally.

"Knowing how much my family means to me, and how lucky I am to be able to see them any time I want to, I also know how much it must be killing you to be so far away from yours."

I am almost ready to cry when he says that. I have tried very hard not to complain to him about how much I miss my parents and my sisters. I have told him often how lucky I feel just to be able to talk with them on the phone. But I know he can see how much I miss them and worry about them and want to be with them. I see how close he is to his own family, and it makes me feel very special that he wants me to have this closeness, too.

It seems incredible to me now that we could go so quickly from such a sweet moment to what comes next.

The fight starts when the bill for our meal arrives. Lupe, our wild and crazy waitress, has been running around the room *como alma que lleva el diablo*, except with a smile that never leaves her face, to wait on so many tables at once that it almost makes me dizzy. Everywhere she goes, bursts of laughter follow. She's having more fun at work than anyone I have ever seen. It's almost as if she's at a party instead of a job. As good as I thought I was at *my* job, I am getting a lesson from a true professional tonight. She extends our bill toward Eduardo with a big smile while calling back over her shoulder a Not Safe for Work answer to another customer. Even though I had told him that I was paying tonight, Eduardo reaches for the bill and for his wallet. I put my hand on his arm to stop him.

"My treat tonight, remember?"

"I know how much Clara pays you and how much you send home. Let me take care of this."

I am glad that Lupe has moved on to another table. I frown at him and hold my hand out, almost in his face.

"At least let me pay my share," he says. "I ate way more than you."

"Please give me the bill and put your wallet away."

I guess I speak to him more sharply than I ever have before. Actually, I don't remember ever raising my voice with him before, at least since that first time we met when I told him not to kick Tyreke when he was on the ground. I don't remember even frowning at him before. In his eyes I can see now that I have seriously hurt his feelings. He looks like a puppy that has been hit with a stick after trying to lick his master's face. He hands me the bill and puts his wallet away. I pay, in cash of course, and leave a good tip for Lupe. When she scoops up the bills and we get up to go, she tries another smile on Eduardo, who sort of looks away instead of returning it. She shrugs and gives me a big hug.

That is more than he gives me when he drops me off at home after silence in the car. The goodnight kiss is just a peck, nothing like what I have come to expect and enjoy. He is punishing me, I think, because I have wounded his pride—just as he wounded mine. I work and earn money, too, and I can pay for a meal! For more than two hundred years his family has lived here in the United States, but I can see now for the first time that the old *machismo* from Mexico is baked into his genes.

I am still crying a little bit when I tell Tori about it later. She rolls her eyes at me as if I have lost my mind.

"If that's the first—or the worst—fault you can find with your man, that he wants to pay the bill when it comes, you better take a good look around and see what other fools be doin' to piss off their women. You got you some kind of a damn prince from another planet where they got grown-ass men, you ask me. Maybe I take him off your hands after all, you got too much pride to let him buy you din-din."

"He's bought me lots of dinners. I just wanted to pay for one." I start to cry harder.

"You know I'm just playin' with you. He a little too short to look good on me anyway." She gives me the hug he gypped me of. I guess it's my night to get love only from my own kind. "Don't give up after one damn fight."

For the rest of the night I carry my phone around in my hand, hoping he will call. He doesn't. When I go to bed, an hour later than usual, I leave it on just in case. I toss and turn for another hour. I'm finally almost asleep when I hear the ping. I snatch the phone to read his text. If I still believed in God, I would be praying that Eduardo isn't going to break up with me this way.

My heart is pounding like crazy, and I can hardly even breathe until I read what he has written:

please forgive me, im an idiot

thank you for dinner, it was great

ps i love u

I stare at the last line for a long time, then put my head back on my pillow, my phone clasped over my heart. This is the first time he has used these words with me. I have heard them more than once from other guys, but this is the first time I want to say them back. I will not do it in a text message, though.

I will tell him to his face tomorrow.

CHAPTER 44

MOUA

So I didn't get kicked out of school after all. I got kicked out of the house instead.

What happened was the g-ma was poking around when she should have been minding her own business instead of mine, and she heard me on the phone. You'll never guess with who: her favorite guy in the whole wide world. I was just getting him off and pretending to get off myself when she pulled open the door to my room and caught me in the act, so to speak. People seem to think it was what happened to Martha that gave the g-ma her second stroke, but I think it was probably me handing her the phone and asking if she wants to speak to Pastor Greg after he pulls up his pants.

I'd passed on trying to get Professor Bisson to avail himself of my services, but after what I'd heard from Morgan about the horndog preacher who tried to squeeze her tits while he was saving her soul, I saw another opportunity. I almost offered to teach her the ropes of the phone sex trade, give her a useful skill, but I didn't trust her enough to take her into the biz, so instead I decided to see if I could cash in myself. I gave him a call and left my number, with a message that couldn't be mistaken. He was on it almost right away, and he quickly became a regular. You can tell from his voice how desperate he is. He has all kinds of disgusting ideas. I won't waste your time with the details about what he wants to do to my body: let's just say the J-man had more fun up on the cross. This pastor probably belongs behind bars instead of behind a pulpit, but my phone service and the Sunday rub-a-dubs with the titwits in his church might just be enough to keep him out of prison. Maybe I'll record him next time and threaten to play it back for the adoring members of his congregation, if the g-ma hasn't recovered enough to have him cashiered by then. I'll bet I can squeeze an extra payment out of his donation box.

The g-ma sort of started frothing at the mouth when I offered her the phone, so that's when I called 9-1-1. She had already been acting really weird since the pit bull tried to eat Martha and the baby, like that was going to finish her off, and I guess maybe this put her over the top. Anyway, the ambulance came and took her to the hospital. A couple of days later I found out she was coming home, I was getting evicted, and the g-pa was moving out of the garage and into my room to take care of her. That social worker Ms. Robinson for some reason kept in touch with them after the adoption plan fell through, and she even found a way for him to get paid for providing live-in care, so he actually has a job now. I wish she had found a way to pay *me* for doing the poop duty. I can hardly wait to hear how the g-pa does with that.

For a minute there after I got kicked out, I was homeless. No way was I moving back into the prison cell at my mom's house. Luckily, I had some money saved up from my enterprise and was able to get another room in an apartment really quickly with another girl in one of my classes. Her previous roommate moved in with her boyfriend out of the blue and skipped out on her share of last month's rent, so she was glad to accommodate me. The first thing I did after I moved in was to put a lock on my bedroom door.

So I guess you figured out I took the crappy deal Booker Bisson offered me. That temporary F I'm stuck with isn't going to help me get into the nursing program, that's for sure, but I'm starting seriously to think about changing my major anyway. Like Alicia suggested, business might work out a little better for someone with my skill set. All those days I spent steering the g-ma's wheelchair and cleaning up her messes taught me just as much as anything I ever learned in any class. I think maybe I'm cut out more for using my brain to make a living. I've got my own Web site now, and I'm expanding my current operation. I'm thinking of putting up a photo of Tori in her Roadhouse glory, to get guys thinking they're putting it to her when they're on the phone with me. Maybe I'll even photoshop that Aung San Suu Kyi into a g-string, cash in on her looks, too. You never know: someday they might give out a Nobel Prize for Pornography, and I'll be first in line. It's something to shoot for anyway. The counselors at school are always telling us how important it is to have goals, right?

The other thing that happened is my sister texted me to let me know that Mr. Vang called her to get my phone number—not for what you're thinking, though. When she got the call, she was hoping he was going to propose to my mom or arrange to kidnap her and trade in a few goats, but it turns out that he just wants to offer me a job. It seems he got hired to teach a class here at the college, on top of all his high school classes, and the college gives him some money to hire an assistant to grade papers or tutor some of the dummies. He tried to tell me back in high school that I'd make a good math teacher, so I guess this is his way of following up on that idea. You can understand that it's not exactly my dream come true. According to Tori, teachers are like one step above garbage collectors. On the other hand, it's one of the few professions that still has decent benefits and a pension, and, like that journalism teacher at my high school proved, it's really hard to get yourself fired, no matter how hard you try. So it might be worth considering. I do get tired of listening all day to perverts like Pastor Greg telling me what they want to do to me. So I may call Mr. V back, just to see what the job pays, anyway. I won't tell him how much I'm making now or what I'm doing. Unless, of course, the conversation takes a turn in that direction. You never know where the next porn opp may pop up.

Even if you don't really give a crap about what's going on with some Hmong girl you never met (but might have talked to on the phone), you probably want to hear about what happened with everybody else. I found out after I went back to pick up

some of my stuff that I left behind when I got kicked out. So
Alicia didn't get to keep her baby after all, but she says she'll
keep trying to get custody of her, no matter what the medical
issues are and no matter how long it takes. It won't be easy, but
I wouldn't bet against her. I wouldn't bet against her becoming
a doctor, either. Even with everything she took on this semester,
working for Clara and taking care of Brianna and trying to help
Morgan and Martha and dating Eduardo, she still got straight
A's. She even seems to have found a guy who's not an asshole,
which is way harder than getting a 4.0. He planted a tree for her
in the g-ma's backyard, and from the way those two lovebirds go
around each other at school all goo-goo eyed and holding hands
and all that other yucky PDA stuff, you can tell they'll probably
be getting married and popping out some babies of their own
before too long.

Alicia and Eduardo aren't the only ones probably getting
married. Crazy old Clara is engaged again, to some guy she met
who runs the Food Bank. Alicia says the guy is really fat but
really nice, which is sort of what you'd expect to hear about
someone who spends his whole life giving out free food. She's
sure he's a huge improvement on the deadbeats Clara picked
before. Clara tells her third time's the cure, fourth time's the
charm. We'll see about that.

Tori is another candidate for a meal-ticket merger. Like me,
she's rethinking the whole nursing thing, especially after that
big fat D she wound up with in Chemistry. I told her she's lucky
I didn't rat her out and give her half of my F in History, too. I
think she's pretty jealous of Alicia for hooking up with Eduardo.
She might even have learned something there. She says her new
plan is to speak softly and marry a big dick. She's narrowing
her date-search to this year's draft choices by the 49ers and the
Warriors. I told her she'd better make sure she gets a no-cut
contract.

Baby Bri is being taken care of temporarily by some couple
that specializes in at-risk babies, so I guess maybe for the time
being this whole deal worked out okay for her—other than

having half of her stomach chomped out, of course. Alicia has arranged to visit her and invited me to come along. We'll see about that, too. It's not exactly the highest priority on my list right now. I'll probably go along just to keep Alicia company, but sometimes I can't help thinking Brianna would have been a lot better off if we'd never gotten involved in trying to help her in the first place.

Martha kept her arm but lost the eye. That's going to make studying for school even tougher for her, of course, and she was no speed-reader to begin with. She somehow passed that math class she was taking for the fourth time with the lowest possible C on the final exam. I'm sure she's giving the credit to the G-man, but the four hours or so that Alicia and I spent cramming with her in the library the night before the test just might have had something to do with it, too. I wasn't too thrilled about it when Alicia called me to set up the study session, but it didn't kill me, and I had the night free anyway since there was no point in studying for my final in history. I guess you could say it was good practice in case I take Mr. V up on his offer: if I can help Martha pass math, I can probably help just about anyone.

Like Tori and me, I think Martha's also about ready to bail on nursing. She even asked me about switching to business and learning how to invest in the stock market; she really bought that cover story I sold her, and since the g-ma can't talk now, she couldn't set her straight. Imagine Martha's surprise if I tell her how I'm really making money. But, come to think of it, if they've got Christian rap at her church now, how much of a stretch would it be to Christian porn? I won't be able to put her face up on my Web site anytime soon, of course, until after she has some more surgery. Just have to go with a body shot for now. She can borrow a top from Tori and dangle that necklace with the big crucifix on it down in the valley, like lots of the girls at school do. Pastor Greg will be creaming before he even picks up the phone.

Besides passing math, one other good thing that came out of all this is Martha lost about forty pounds, which is what sucking all of your food through a straw for a month or two will do for you. Knowing her, I'm sure she'll chalk up her new figure to divine intervention, too. At least when she looks in the mirror now, she sees a skinny girl who was mangled by a pit bull instead of a fat one.

Those cops that rescued Martha and Bri from the pit bull were in the news a few days ago. Twice actually. Maybe you even saw the video on TV or Facebook of the first time. They were called in to a robbery-in-progress at a liquor store, not far from Clara's restaurant. Some guy in the parking lot got the whole thing on his phone. One thief is in the store when Officer Mason goes in after him. His accomplice is in the parking lot, but the cops don't spot him. He somehow gets behind Officer Santos and gets her gun away from her. Then he's pointing it at her head and telling Officer Mason to drop his gun when Mason comes out of the store with the other guy. You can hear the guy with her gun on the video talking to her. It's really gross. He's obviously high on something and he's saying he's going to rape her and cut her tits off and then stuff them down her throat. He asks Officer Mason if he wants to watch, then tells him again to drop his gun. Officer Mason raises his gun instead and shoots the guy in the face. Officer Santos grabs her own gun back as the guy is going down, dead before he hits the ground, and she shoots the guy who had been in the store. Officer Mason had already disarmed him. It was hard to tell from the video, but a couple of witnesses say it looked like the guy was trying to run away, so I guess she might get in some trouble for that, especially if the guy dies.

Their second time in the news came the next day. Some girl who saw the video from the liquor store recognized Officer Mason and identified him as the cop who pressured her for *favors* after he busted her for possession at her high school. She was like seventeen at the time. So Officer Mason goes in twenty-four hours from being the hero who stopped a robbery and saved his partner's life to being the scumbag who can't keep his hands off underage girls. Of course, she could be making the whole thing up, like I thought about doing with Professor Bisson, but she sounded pretty convincing when they interviewed her on TV. So he's probably another guy who could have benefited, maybe even saved his career, by giving me a call.

Before they got famous, the cops tracked down Morgan. They didn't recover Clara's cash or Alicia's locket or anything of Tori's. Morgan made up some fairy tale about a customer coming into the café and hitting the register while she was on the hopper. She claimed that the other girls told her she could borrow anything she wanted from their rooms, but she lost their stuff when *she* was robbed on the street by some homeless guy. She also said she'd purposely left Brianna in our care, which I suppose was the only part of her story that was close to being true. Some judge ate the whole thing up with a spoon and gave her probation. Meanwhile, it turns out she'd already got back with Tyreke. She had been staying with him at his mother's duplex, and she was the one who forgot to lock the gate that the pit bull got out from before it attacked Martha and Bri—or at least that's what she testified in court. Maybe she said that just to get Tyreke off the hook. Whatever the truth might have been, the judge in that case didn't sentence either one of them, I guess because nobody died (although the g-ma came close, thanks to me) except the dog. Tyreke replaced his pit bull with a Doberman and a Rottweiler.

If that isn't exactly the happy-ever-after you were hoping for, check this out. Morgan tells Tyreke about stealing the stuff from the g-ma's house, and he decides to pay a visit one night, see if there's anything marketable that Morgan missed. He breaks a window and gets in, no problem. He makes it to the g-ma's room, where she's snoring away, seriously medicated from like every drug in the world. You couldn't wake her up with a firehose up her nose. Again, perfect for Tyreke. He grabs some jewelry, starts back out. He gets back to the window to hand the stuff out to Morgan, only it isn't her waiting there for him. It's the g-pa, with his shotgun loaded with buckshot.

I imagine you can picture for yourself how that turned out.

QUESTIONS FOR DISCUSSION

1. The novel focuses on students who are working their way through college. Compare their experiences at work and at school with your own or with those of others you have known.

2. Moua and Eduardo have very different experiences as students of Professor Booker Bisson. How did you respond to their interactions with him and his impact on them? Compare or contrast your own experiences with teachers and comment on their role in shaping your attitude toward education.

3. Many of the novel's characters (Alicia, Officer Santos, Moua, Tori, Eduardo, Martha, and Natalie) express their feelings about their parents, while others (Jack, Morgan, Booker, and Clara) express their feelings about their children. Compare their feelings with your own or with those of others you have known.

4. A prominent theme in the novel is the quest for adoption. How did you respond to Alicia's determination to accomplish this, and how did you feel about Natalie's decision to allow a trial period in Violet's household? What challenges does adoption present? Would you consider adoption yourself?

5. The theme of abortion as an alternative to delivering unplanned children is introduced in the recollections of Martha and Natalie. How did you react to the accounts they gave of their own experiences? What do you think you would have done or urged someone you know to do in their circumstances?

6. The issue of religious faith or lack thereof is foreshadowed in the epigraph from Lorraine Hansberry's *A Raisin in the Sun*, developed in sections narrated by Martha and Violet and in a conversation between Alicia and Eduardo, reprised in comments by Jack and Natalie, and extended in the depiction of Pastor Greg. How did you respond to the novel's presentation of this issue, and how do the beliefs and values of various characters compare or contrast with your own?

7. As with religion, consideration of the topic of politics is often discouraged, but this novel invites readers to compare or contrast their own political leanings with those of the characters. Multiple characters express their contempt for President Trump, while Martha defends him. Which comments on this impeached figure resonated with you?

8. Police officers and ex-soldiers are among the characters playing key roles in this novel. How did you respond to the characterizations of Officer Mason, Officer Santos, Eduardo Martinez, and Jack Mackey? How did the conduct of these characters compare or contrast with that of cops or soldiers you have known or known about?

9. The novel has a diverse cast of characters, including representation of a Native American (Clara, who also has traces of other races), blacks (Tori, Tyreke, Natalie, Booker) whites (Officer Mason, Martha, Jack, Morgan, Violet), and Asians (Moua, Officer Santos). What attitudes expressed by any of the characters about racial issues stood out? Compare or contrast your own experiences with people from ethnic backgrounds different from your own and the role of these experiences in shaping your own values regarding race.

10. Martha, Eduardo, and Booker make brief references to contemporary music. How did you react to their comments, and what is your own opinion of the merits of hip hop?

11. The novel has many references to movies and even includes a character, Eduardo, who would like to make them. Which references to movies did you recognize, and what was their significance? Compare or contrast this book with films you have seen.

12. By some estimates, one-fourth of all students attending community colleges have experienced homelessness. Several characters in the novel make reference to the impact of this issue. Identify and comment on these references and then explain your own relevant feelings. What is local government doing to help the homeless? What can individuals do about this problem?

13. What impact did the inclusion of dogs in this novel have on you? How did you respond to the flashback involving Martha and her grandfather and the later incident involving Martha and Brianna? What experiences have you had with animals, and how do they compare or contrast with the experiences described in the novel? What is your opinion of legislation that bans restrictions on private ownership of attack dogs?

14. Among other genres, this novel is in part a love story. How did you respond to the development of a romantic relationship between Alicia and Eduardo? What traits or values do you think brought them together? Compare or contrast their relationship with other pairings noted in the novel and/or with the beginnings of your own primary romantic relationship.

15. Apart from the obvious examples of Alicia and Eduardo, with which character were you most sympathetic? Why? With which character were you least sympathetic? Why?

16. What specific scene or conversation in the novel was most relevant to your own life, in the form of either a comparison or a contrast? Why?

17. What is the significance of the final gesture attributed by Moua to Natalie?

18. What do you think is the most important theme in this novel?

19. This novel has an open ending of the kind that Tori decries in movies, with the last line leaving the reader's finger on the trigger. Moua gets the last word, summarizing or projecting outcomes for some characters but leaving others up in the air. What other choices for the final narrative section might the author have made? Write an alternate ending in the voice of one of the other characters.

20. Read the poems that follow these questions and connect them with characters and events in the novel.

A STOCKTON HERO

My friend Cenon,
With a smile on his face,
Empties the trash from my basket,
Asks me how I'm doing, chides me if I'm working late,
Calls me still, after all these years, "Mr. Phil,"
As if I were somehow his better.

This from a man,
My friend Cenon, who served three tours in Vietnam,
Not on desk duty, not typing inflated tallies of enemies slain,
Nor ordering others into chaos from the comfort of remote command,
But in the shit every day, death and dismemberment a misstep away,
With the 3rd Marine Division.

While I was groaning over Melville in an air-conditioned carrel,
He patrolled the jungles, in constant peril,
My friend Cenon, finding ways to stay alive,
And helping the less-seasoned to survive.
As I fussed over footnotes and bibliography tags,
He sent brothers home in pieces or in bags.

Like his father, who fought the imperial killers of Japan
As a guerrilla in the Philippines,
But said little of the horrors he had known,
My friend Cenon is just glad he made it home.
When I press for more of his war and his fate,
He turns the topic, tells me again not to work too late.

This from a man who took a full-time job
At Delta College, another at Linden High,
Not so nearby, and between them put in
Eighty hours a week, for twenty-eight years.
My friend Cenon, cleaning up messes the rest of us left
To give to his children the chances he missed.

When colleagues complain of PTSD from "too many papers to grade,"
I think about this quiet man and the double-duty he took on,
Atop his three tours, and the three kids he raised,
And how much I will miss him when he is gone,
With a smile on his face,
My hero, Mr. Cenon.

This poem was originally published in *Soundings Magazine*
(https://soundingsmag.net), February 2019.

A DOCTOR SOMEDAY

First in his clan to come to college,
First, in fact, to finish grade ten,
At age twelve, Daniel one day followed his father
Into fields to harvest in heat that reached 103 degrees.
Afterward, his father said, "Is what your life will be
Si you no stay in school."

Daniel is nobody's fool.
He paid attention to his dad, pays attention in my class,
Shows *respeto*, no buds in his ears, no phone in his grasp
Or, like his peers, cleverly concealed upon his lap.
He follows directions, works through multiple drafts,
Proofreads and edits, hands in on time.
By the siren call of the semicolon Daniel is not seduced:
His sentences are sound, make sense, do not run-on
Or stop halfway to their intended destination.
In class he is quiet, seldom volunteers,
Keeps it short when called upon,
Perhaps embarrassed by an accent's trace,
But always ready with an answer.
He's confounded now and then, as are the best of men
By the nuances of pronoun case:
(Even our eloquent ex-President, Columbia and Harvard behind,
Once began "Her and Biden can . . ." on a televised show;
Given the forty million or so added to the health care rolls,
I almost manage to let it go.)
When I pass back a perfect test
Or an essay dense with details and insights
Surprising from one so young, to myself I say,
"This kid knows his shit."
Daniel will be a doctor someday.

After class he lingers one day,
Waits patiently for others to grub for grades,
Bury bonus grandmothers, or razz me about the 49ers' latest fade.
When the classroom clears, he thanks me for my corrections,
Then confesses fears for his career,
Not sure he can hack the math to get there.
Numbers were never my friend,
But, even with no way of knowing where this will end,
I say right away, "You can do it,"
Somewhere in my bones feeling that the same *fuerza*
That fueled a father through twelve-hour days

To feed his family will sustain his son
Through calculus and organic chem, med school and beyond.
We talk of tutors, scholarships, GPA and T-A-G.
He thanks me again for encouraging him, offers a tamale
Home-made by his mom, who still packs a lunch to send along.
When I ask about his coming Christmas break,
I learn of plans, now, alas, aborted by border-crossing fears,
To go to Mexico, not to bask on the beach at Cancun or Cabo,
But to build with his church a house
That three families, now homeless, would have shared
In the town where his father was born,
Where a man works a week or more
To earn what I am paid for an hour.
Though I share not a whit of his theosophy,
He gives me faith of a different kind,
And I'm just glad his life touched mine.

When he walks out the door after the final exam,
On his way to Davis or Berkeley or UCLA,
Chances are I will never see him again.
Just maybe, though, this *prodigio* I teach
Exceeds his reach, becomes the surgeon,
World class, who pioneers a new technique,
Performs the transplant I'm sure to need
After reading so much of his classmates' trash
Has turned my brain to succotash.
Either way, he'll be okay.
Even if the lout in the White House now
Manages to deports him, somehow,
Some way, Daniel will be a doctor someday.

This poem was originally published in *Soundings Magazine*
(https://soundingsmag.net), March 2020.

IN PRAISE OF HARD WORK

(Composed for the memorial service of Ian Douglass Hutcheon)

"Far and away the best prize that life has to offer is the chance to
work hard at work worth doing."

—Theodore Roosevelt

Obituaries never tell the whole story.
My brother, man of many accomplishments,
Worked to track down terrorists
From fragments of the bombs they left behind.
He helped to make the world a little safer
For the rest of us, blessed with less stressful lives.
My brother, man of few words,
Sworn to secrecy, kept his vow,
Revealed no details while he drew breath.
Few came forth when he died.
I know only the barest bones:
How hard he worked,
How far he strove
To be, if not always the smartest guy in the room,
Always the one who could be counted on
To get the job done,
No matter the time,
No matter the toll.
Fighting diabetes, anemia, and cancer along the way,
To get to his desk or his lab every day.
Thanks for all the hard work, brother.

Author's note: My mother, Louise Hansen Hutcheon, worked full-
time to age seventy-eight, then spent the next five years voluntarily
caring for a neighboring single-father's son. When her health then
declined, my sister Marilyn and our younger brother Todd took care
of her in the house we grew up in. I chipped in on weekends. After
Mom died, at home, in my sister's arms, at age ninety-one, our brother
Ian said, "Thanks for all the hard work," which I recognized as the
highest praise possible in his lexicon. This poem was my attempt to
return the compliment.

AN INTERVIEW WITH THE AUTHOR

1. Your first three novels focused on basketball, football, and baseball, respectively. What led you to tackle a topic so different from the subjects of your previous books in this one?

I guess the most honest answer is that I ran out of sports. Some readers expressed frustration with my focus on ballgames and challenged me to try something new. I always learn a lot from and about my students, so I decided to try to write a book focused on them. Many of them are first-generation college students from families who immigrated in recent years. Reading about and seeing on television news stories about the infants being separated from their immigrant parents at the border now supplied the impetus to get started.

2. What were your most important literary sources for this novel?

The narrative technique was inspired by Faulkner's *As I Lay Dying*. I got from this novel about the tortuous journey to bury a family member the notion of using short chapters with multiple narrators, some of them unsympathetic or unreliable, to weave together from diverse perspectives the various strands of the story of the adoption quest. I can also attribute in part to this book the element of farce, which is seldom far from my consciousness, and the focus on the hypocrisy of religious leaders in mine. The surname of the hands-on pastor in my novel is a nod to Faulkner's randy reverend.

The theme of "the circle of duty," focusing on the problems right in front of us, comes straight from *Bleak House*, in which Dickens memorably ridiculed investment in "telescopic philanthropy" in his era, while London's poor were dying in the streets. Elmore Leonard, "the Dickens of Detroit," also has influenced everything I have written with his inspired dialog and this timeless advice: "Try to leave out the part that readers tend to skip." And I borrowed from Edward Albee's Martha for my own the alchemy of revirginization. I realize, of course, that I am an ant inching at the base of the peaks crested by these masters. I figure it can't hurt to learn from the best.

3. Are you concerned that the Part I epigraph from Hansberry's *A Raisin in the Sun* might prevent some readers from getting past those words to page one of this novel?

I completed an undergraduate major in French and read extensively in Existentialism, but as a young adult no passage in Camus or Sartre hit me as hard as the lines I quoted from Hansberry's play. The speech by Beneath Younger struck me like a lightning bolt when I first read it. Her words preface the conversation between Alicia and Eduardo that places those two characters outside of conventional morality. I recognize that some devout readers, including some of my friends, my colleagues, and my students, may be offended. While I respect everyone's right to worship as they see fit, as long their religions do not violate the human rights of others, I have seen some surveys indicating that as many as 30% of Americans now reject theism, and I suspect that the percentage is considerably higher among the educated. I hope that most readers of my book will be open-minded enough to consider a perspective on faith different from their own. I'll concede that after the speech I quoted Beneatha is coerced to repeat, "In my mother's house there is still God," but I'll leave it to readers (or theater-goers) to decide which lines have the greater impact.

4. You take on more than one sacred cow here: you also have numerous political references in your book. What were your intentions there?

A purveyor of fiction would be hard-pressed to (pardon the expression) trump the daily outrages of our post-Obama surreality show. I often hear college students say that they aren't interested in or don't care about politics. I understand that they are busy with school and work and families, and trying to squeeze in some fun, as I was (well, except for the "fun" part) at their age, but I hope to inspire a few readers to pay a little more attention to the fate of our democracy, or maybe even inspire the Republicans among them to look into The Lincoln Project. I especially hope that any Christians who make it past the Hansberry epigraph might be moved to reconsider whether they should be supporting, on the single-issue basis of his shamelessly pragmatic opposition to abortion, a twice-divorced serial philanderer whose life has been characterized by repeated sexual harassment (or worse), race-baiting, corruption, fraud, extortion, and name-calling on a level more befitting an ill-parented third grader than the President of the United States. I also wanted to remind readers who might not have been alive then of an earlier era when the course of our nation's history was profoundly altered, and an opportunity for a different kind of world at the dawn of the twenty-first century was squandered, by another impeached President's concupiscence and pathetic attempt to cover it up.

5. Apart from the narrative technique, how was the process of writing this book different from writing your previous books?

The main differences are that this novel is half as long, and I wrote the first draft much faster. Faulkner famously claimed that he wrote *As I Lay Dying* in six weeks, writing from midnight to four a.m. after working all day in a power plant, and I drew inspiration from this account, however hyperbolic it might be. I fiddled with my first novel for twenty years before it finally was published, and the next two each required several years from gestation through research to publication. I wrote *A Child Left Behind* essentially in two stretches when I wasn't teaching full-time (and minus the power plant), in 2019. As soon as I finished a narrative section, it seemed to lead inexorably to the next; I hadn't had that experience before.

Since I was writing about college students and hoping to interest some of them as readers, I decided that a novel shorter than my previous books would be a good idea, given how busy students are balancing school with work and family obligations— and how much they lament lengthy reading assignments.

6. As in your previous books, you use movie references frequently again in this novel. Can you explain why?

Movies continue to have a major impact on shaping my sense of ways to tell stories. With their diverse casts and intersecting plotlines, *Crash* and *Syriana* are models I have drawn from. Any writer could take a lesson from the use of a critical flashback in *Blindspotting* or *Three Billboards outside Ebbing, Missouri.* Asghar Farhadi's *A Separation* shows the impact of Alzheimer's Disease on a family in a more compelling way than any book I've read on the subject. *Cadillac Records*, for which Beyoncé and director Darnell Martin should have had Academy Award nominations, entertainingly educated millions of Americans about African American musicians. *Beyond Rangoon* gave the world a compelling glimpse of the heroism of Aung San Suu Kyi. Movies like *We Were Soldiers* and *Rio Bravo* are part of the bonding experience that links generations. The recognition of Mexican directors in recent years by the Motion Picture Academy is a step forward in promoting equality of opportunity in the film industry, although of course, as Eduardo notes in the novel, there is still a long way to go in this country in creating a fair representation of all of the kinds of people who make up our society. Eduardo may choose nursing, history, botany, or business instead, but I'm hoping more people like him will get a chance to make movies.

For all of his many well-publicized faults, Frank Sinatra was an early and active supporter of Martin Luther King, Jr., and left a legacy of racial egalitarianism evident in many of the film roles that he chose. Witness his delivery, with utter conviction, of this line from *Never So Few* (from the novel by Thomas Chamales), to an American World War II medical officer ignoring the needs of his wounded or sick Kachin allies in the battle against Imperial Japan: "Your kind of so-called democratic American burns my butt." Those words gave me a *frisson* when I first heard them at age ten, and they still resonate. We seem to need their reminder more than ever now.

7. Also as in your previous novels, cops and soldiers—or ex-soldiers—figure prominently in this one. Can you account for this recurring pattern?

I am profoundly grateful for the service and the sacrifice of those who put their lives on the line in professions far more perilous than mine—to give bookworms like me the liberty to portray them, warts and all. People like Officer Mason and Jack Mackey are part of our country, and we need to be aware of their contributions as well as of their limitations. I also wanted to acknowledge those, like Eduardo's family members, who are doing something more than just talking about helping the wounded veterans to whom we all owe so much.

My now retired Delta College co-worker Cenon Fusco was the model for Eduardo's great-grandfather and grandfather. Cenon served three tours in Vietnam with the 3rd Marine Division and then worked two full-time jobs for twenty-eight years to give his kids opportunities unavailable to him. Captain Travis Nolen of the 7th Air Cavalry visited my class to discuss his experiences in Vietnam, where he won the Bronze Star and Silver Star—then, like John Kerry, threw them away. He was the source of the incident described by Jack Mackey when a Viet Cong soldier stepped on his hand but did not discover him. Naval veteran Danny McConnell provided the story from a comrade about the Viet Cong's slitting of throats in the tent on his first night in country.

8. What personal connections do you have with some of the other characters you've depicted?

The students in the novel are amalgams of various women and men who have been in my classes, and many of the events these characters describe are either closely or loosely based on events that my students have written about in their essays or talked about in class discussions.

Clara Birdsong is based in part on the woman who was my first boss. Like many white Americans of my generation, I went through high school, college, and graduate school without ever having a black teacher. After a privileged childhood that did not require me to hold a job, during my first year of college, like Booker in the novel, I took any jobs I could get to begin to pay my way. The first of these was as a hasher in a sorority house. My supervisor there was an African-American woman.

Her name was Earlene Webb, and I learned as much from her as in any of my classes. Most of the women in the sorority were pleasant and respectful, but a few were archetypal princesses who wanted to tell the peons how to do our jobs. Earlene let me know right away that I had to stand up for myself—and showed me exactly how to do it. She didn't take any guff from anyone, nor did she let anyone abuse me. She didn't put up with any nonsense from me, either. After a couple of times when I was a few minutes late to work, she told me straight up, "If you want to keep this job and work for me, you have to be here on time." The next day I showed up probably half an hour early; she laughed and said, "Just on time, okay?" In all the years since then, I've never had a better or more memorable mentor.

My Hansen cousins and their patriarch George provided the model of care for an ailing family member that Eduardo ascribes to his uncle's family. Kathi Duffel at Bear Creek High School is the heroically iconoclastic journalism teacher who inspired events described by Moua. A few other characters are also based on fellow teachers. Booker Bisson's surname is in honor of too-soon-departed Delta College history professor Joe Bisson, who challenged political correctness at every turn. The basketball coach to whom Booker refers, Hubert "Camp" Pendleton, also appears in my first novel and is based on my Menlo College colleague Bud Presley, the stalwart credited by no less an authority than Rick Barry with teaching the Warriors how to play defense during their 1975 championship season. Moua's high school math teacher Mr. Vang is modeled after Mike Thibodeaux, also formerly my colleague at Menlo College, and by far the best teacher in any subject that I have ever known. The story of Mr. Vang's witnessing at age six his mother's execution came directly from a survivor of the Khmer Rouge in one of the first classes that I taught at Delta.

9. Authors often say that asking them to choose a favorite among their characters is like asking parents to choose among their children, but . . . do you have a favorite character in this novel or one with whom you identify most closely?

I imagine some readers who know me would connect me through *the old guard* with Booker, although I lack the distinction of the Civil Rights activist background I gave him. I do share some of his values and his frustrations, but I am less invested in the sanctity of any curricula I had a hand in, and I'm more receptive to the energy and enthusiasm of a new generation of teachers. Although I don't share Moua's view of the value of a C in my English 1A class, in some ways she is the character whose sensibility is closest to my own. Perhaps that's why she gets the longest section as well as the last one. As a reflection of the culture that my students are growing up in, it's also worth noting that Moua knows who Stormy Daniels is but not who Aung San Suu Kyi is. In Alicia I was aiming to create a woman readers could fall in love with, and in Eduardo a suitor worthy of her devotion. The characters I had the most fun writing were Tori and Jack, probably because their thoughts and speech are unfiltered. But my favorite character is Natalie. In her I was trying for a woman who wrestles with a hard decision that results in a failure and then has to figure out how to deal with it. Failure is a big part of all of our lives. It certainly has been a big part of mine. I console myself by recalling that even the greatest hitters in baseball history failed to reach base more often than they succeeded (Ted Williams came closest to the fifty/fifty split at .482), and even Michael Jordan failed to win the NBA championship in more seasons (9) than he won it (6). What matters most to me is how we handle our setbacks. Through the small act of generosity that Moua reports at the end of the novel, Natalie shows that in spite of her failures she has not given up on trying to help others— irrespective of race or background— which I hope is ultimately what this novel is about. Anyone who writes about race and depicts racist characters runs the risk of being labeled a racist himself or herself, but I hope readers will see in Natalie's core values some of my own.

10. Why did you choose to set this novel in a community college?

A few years ago a silver-spoonfed Southern California

legislator grabbed some headlines during state budgetary wars by claiming that nobody successful ever came from a community college. The California Community Colleges are the largest public education system in the world. We have our share of failures, to be sure, but we also have many success stories. As Booker and Moua discuss, one of them is Dolores Huerta, who was awarded the Presidential Medal of Freedom for her Civil Rights activism. Another noteworthy example, as told in *Becoming Dr. Q*, is Alfredo Quinones-Hinojosa, who passed through Delta College on his path from migrant farm work to neurosurgery. We celebrate our quarterbacks more than our brain surgeons, so a more famous example is Aaron Rodgers of the Green Bay Packers, who started his journey to the NFL's Hall of Fame at Butte College. In recent years he donated a million dollars to help the victims of fires in Northern California.

An example more directly relevant to my life is my own immigrant father, Ian L. Hutcheon, who lost *his* father in early childhood and his mother in his teens, then, like Dolores Huerta, attended Stockton College, earning a scholarship to the College (now University) of the Pacific. There he led the tennis team to its first Far Western Conference championships, prior to serving in the U.S. Navy during World War II. Piloting a PB-Y that had been declared obsolete before the war ever began and facing Japanese Zeroes with more than twice its airspeed, he won a Distinguished Flying Cross and kept his crew alive through two years of combat. Later he spent thirty years in public education, rising to the level of superintendent, helping thousands of children along the way and paying special attention to those most in need. At the end of his long life of service, several people who had been students fifty years earlier from what were then called "broken homes" tracked him down, from cities hundreds of miles away, to thank him in person for providing some stability at crucial junctures in their lives. If that isn't a success story, I don't know what is.

I admire very much the students with the talent and dedication to get into Harvard or Stanford or UC Berkeley on the first bounce; I admire just as much those who start at a community college, take any job or jobs they can find to cover their expenses, and fight their way through any obstacles in their path to achieve their education and pursue their dreams. I wrote this book for them.

RECOMMENDATIONS FOR FURTHER READING

For those who enjoyed this book (and even for those who did not), the author recommends the following novels with an academic setting.

1. William Hogan, *The Quartzsite Trip*
2. Kingsley Amis, *Lucky Jim*
3. Richard Russo, *Straight Man*
4. David Lodge, *Changing Places*
5. Michael Chabon, *Wonder Boys*
6. Zadie Smith, *On Beauty*
7. Erik Tarloff, *The Man Who Wrote the Book*
8. Julie Schumaker, *The Shakespeare Requirement*
9. Steven Carter, *Famous Writers School*
10. Malcolm Bradbury, *The History Man*
11. Finally, one for the children is Raymond Abrashkin and Jay Williams's classic *Danny Dunn and the Homework Machine*.

ACKNOWLEDGMENTS

Writing a book is the easy part. Getting it into the world is another story altogether. Enduring the contumely of publishers, editors, and agents, many of whom have never authored a book themselves, is part of the drill for almost any writer of fiction who perseveres. I am grateful to my publishers, especially Dr. Robert Katz at Willowgate Press, Diane Smith and Joseph Racca at Tokay Press, and Rich Turner at *Soundings*. Joan Bailey and Ricardo Hernandez helped me to edit this book. Jason Sandoval of *Shade Dzine* designed its eye-catching covers.

I thank as well the book reviewers who have seen fit to read and critique my work. I am especially grateful to James Cox and the *Midwest Book Review* for yeoman support of small press writers like me. I'm also grateful to Romuald Dzemo of *Readers' Favorite*, Molly Culbertson and Christi Lyle-Rasheed of *Manhattan Book Review*, Candace Andrews in *inside english*, and Tony Sauro and Howard Lachtman of *The Record* for their generous evaluations.

I have tried, in epigraphs and in the interview section appearing here, to acknowledge the literary sources that had the greatest impact on this novel. One other book that has influenced all of my efforts as a writer and as a teacher is William Hogan's *The Quartzsite Trip*. Recently, through the intervention of screenwriter Rick Rapoza and Lionsgate producer Jocelyn Sabo, who are collaborating to bring a version of this neglected masterpiece to television, I had the opportunity to spend an hour on the phone with Mr. Hogan. The conversation was one of the most rewarding experiences of my life. I got the chance to tell him that his brilliant, hilarious, and inspiring novel changed my life and the lives of hundreds of students with whom I shared it, including many who confessed that it was the first book they had ever enjoyed or, in some cases, had even finished. I never hit my stride as a teacher until former colleague Don Albers pressed this book into my hands, and, however far short of its level my own efforts have fallen, it has always been in my mind while writing about the sometimes magical (and sometimes not) interaction of students and teachers.

Four transcendent teachers influenced this book and everything else I have written: at San Carlos High School taskmaster Tom Lorenat and the incandescent Virginia O'Hagan (later Virginia Herbert); at Pacific the infinitely patient and thorough Robert Knighton; and at Rice University Walter Isle, who never flaunted his Harvard/Stanford pedigree but simply, selflessly devoted himself to helping novices like me find our path to the literature that we loved best.

Richard Russo's wonderful *Straight Man* includes in Professor Hank Devereaux's interior monolog, about colleague and would-be author Billy Quigley, this epic line: "It's a hell of a fine man who'll write a novel and keep it to himself." Alas, I'm afraid that Billy's a far better man than I am. I have passed my previous efforts to many colleagues and friends, and they contributed to this book by providing encouragement or suggestions for improvement, posting reviews, and/or sharing my books with their students. Among these are Will Agopsowicz, Candace Andrews, Sarah Antinora, Lynn Beck, Bob Bini, Barbara Broer, John Clanton, Josh Crow, Elinor Fox, Jerry Fripp, Lesley Fujii, Norm Gates, David Gouker, Sam Hatch, Ginger Holden, Josh Huff, Jessica Hutton, Julie Jose, Navneet Kaur, Brian Kendrick, Virginia Kyle, Natalie Latteri, Sarah Lawley, Eric MacDonald, Nancy Mangum, Matt Marconi, Mary Fae McKay, Jerry Morgan, Linda Nugent, Diane Oren, Pamela Pan, Reed Peters, Lowell Pratt, Zachary Prince, Bob Rennicks, Rebel Rickansrud, Jack Saunders, Paula Sheil, Mike Thibodeaux, Jeff Topping, James Van Dyke, Kevin Walcott, Patrick Wall, and Jun Wang. I am grateful to all of them.

Old friends who have stayed in touch since childhood or high school have also played a role in keeping me at the keyboard to produce this book. These include Gordie Burton, Jay Goldsmith, Jeff Ludvigson, Mark Shilstone, and Bob Zachary. I'm especially grateful for the support of Dave Humber, my first friend in the world; Robin Fryer, Managing Editor of the International Transactional Analysis Association's newsletter and author of some of my most cherished reviews; and Eleni Panagopoulou, now retired from her post as a professor at the

University of Thessaloniki and a faithful correspondent and critic across the more than half-century since we spent some precious time together.

I have drawn inspiration, too, from the writing of my students, many of whom have published in the excellent campus literary magazine, *Delta Winds*. These include Mohammad Afghani, Michelle Andreeta, Jonathan Bethards, M. Sharon Conley, Julius Durham, Avigail Eve, Eloisa Garcia, Valerie Garcia, Rebecca Goldsmith, Kayla Holdoway, Marla Jenkins (pseudonym), Alia Kawish, Kayla King, Angelica Lopez, Elijah Martinez, Trellin McCoy, Morgan Millunzi-Lasater, Kelly-Ray Morriston, Noun Neth, Tenille Packer, Lequn Peng, Kelley Pheng, Daksha Prasad, Bella Quintanilla, Cara Rappuhn, Rogene Reynolds, Alissa Saaybe, Kayla Sabella-Weaver, Sabrina Sanchez, James Shahan, Layne Silva, Makala Soeur, Christina Teed, James Wilson, Colby Yeager, and Dennis Zevely. It is safe to say that I have learned far more from students like these than I could ever have possibly imparted to them.

Matt Wetstein, now President of Cabrillo College and (unlike some academic administrators I have known) an avid and eclectic reader, gave me a boost with his public support for my previous books. The best writer I know, twice nominated for the Pushcart Prize, Anna Villegas gave me the invaluable suggestion of deviating from my original plan for this book, which had been to use exclusively female narrators. The voices of Officer Mason, Eduardo, Jack Mackey, Booker, and Tyreke sprung from that suggestion (although anyone irked by any or all of these must blame only me). Scott Smith is a Delta College alumnus and former colleague, now (a far cry from the pusillanimous scribes derided by Office Mason) risking his life to report on the chaos in Venezuela as an Associated Press correspondent. He supplied the spark for Alicia's commentary on her mother's fearful perceptions from abroad of the United States. My colleague Manuel Camacho, who made at least one of his several covert trips across the border underneath a truck, was the source for Tori's mention of that intrepid method of immigration. Along with Gillianne Meza, Manuel also gave me some coaching on Spanish idioms for this book, although any errors of that kind are solely my own. Darryl Dawkins (a.k.a. "Chocolate Thunder") inspired Tori's mangled reference to Terrytoons' characters, probably far more familiar to several generations now than are Robert Louis Stevenson's.

My deans, Joe Gonzales and Sheli Ayers, have consistently provided the kind of supportive and spirited leadership that inspires a full-time teacher to maintain an avocation. Shaheen Ayaz, even while caring for her own ailing parents around-the-clock, helped me to cope with the loss of my own, and in the wake of their passing my brother Todd has held our family together, freeing me for more lightsome pursuits.

Finally, I must acknowledge once again Joan Bailey, the beautiful and generous woman with whom it has been my privilege to spend my life. Many years ago, when I first started trying to write fiction, Joan offered to support me if I wanted to write full-time. Given the track record that ensued, it's a good thing that I kept my day job. Nevertheless, I am grateful for her unwavering devotion and encouragement. Anything of worth that I may have written is a reflection of her love for me—and mine for her.

ABOUT THE AUTHOR

Phil Hutcheon grew up in Redwood City, California, with frequent trips through Stockton to visit relatives farming in Linden. His dreams of succeeding Willie Mays in centerfield for the San Francisco Giants dashed when he was cut from the junior high school squad, he turned for consolation to literature. He earned a bachelor's degree from the University of the Pacific and a PhD from Rice University. He teaches composition and film at Delta College, recently ranked by personal finance website WalletHub as the number one community college in California and fourth best in the nation. He has also taught at Pacific and at Menlo College. *A Child Left Behind* is his fourth published novel. Determined to be the last man standing on the planet without a cell phone, a Facebook page, or a Twitter addiction, he will respond to readers who email him at philip. hutcheon@deltacollege.edu with the novel's title or its acronym ACLB in the subject line.

Made in the USA
Columbia, SC
20 September 2020